This is a work of fiction. Names, characters, places, and incidents either are the product of the author's imagination or are used fictitiously. Any resemblance to actual events, locales, organizations, or persons, living or dead, is entirely coincidental and beyond the intent of either the author or the publisher.

Elemental Ops
by Julia Talbot

Elemental Ops

Ice

Teamwork

Found

Vanished

Hunted

Elemental Ops

Ice

Chapter One

Ice stared down the barrel of his rifle, a muscle jumping in his cheek. He had a bad feeling about this mission. Like a really bad one. So bad that he'd left the team behind to a man. Jacques and Gig had protested, but he'd snarled at them just like he'd been snarling since Spider had officially left the group, sniffing after a couple of shifters who seemed to draw him like a moth to the flame.

Although, Spider had been their fire elemental, and it was tough for him to be ice without fire.

The target on this mission was a son of a bitch who was hoarding weaponry of the unusual kind and was classified as Armed and Talented. It had taken Ice a month just to find his hideout. It was a fortress, really, a huge thing built into the side of a mountain. The terrain made recon difficult, all shale and other craggy rock deposits, and the whole place smelled like brimstone, the occasional glow of a fiery light tempting Ice to come in out of the cold. His feet were like blocks of frozen snow, even with toe warmers in his boots.

Ice wasn't sure if the guy had demons in there or maybe just a hole into Hell. That would be interesting…

Whatever it was, the directive had been serious enough about the danger that he'd gone Oscar Mike in the middle of the night, leaving his team behind while they slept. They could go on without him, but he needed them to be safe.

A truck rumbled up toward the place, shocks rattling and shaking over the rough road. Whoever was driving had to be losing his fucking mind. Ice would have left the damned truck and hoofed it in. Lord.

A guy got out when the truck parked -- someone who looked oddly familiar, although he couldn't place the face -- carrying a… pet crate? What the fuck? This was so not a dog rescue or anything. This was a weapons stockpile. Right?

He stared, relaxing his eyes so the scope didn't flatten out his vision.

A lean, mostly naked man with the wildest mass of jet-black hair he'd ever seen came out of the building, peered into the crate. The two men began talking -- maybe negotiating? Hell, this was the most action he'd experienced since he'd been on point. He focused on the truck driver for now, trying to place the man.

The truck driver pulled a piece, drew a bead on the guy, who snorted and stared at the man like he was an idiot, not an ounce of fear on the hawk-like face.

Okay, that was interesting. Ice focused on the other guy for a moment. That fearless bastard stirred something like admiration in him. That mostly naked body stirred something a little farther south.

The pistol was grabbed, tossed away, then the pet carrier was snatched up and the man headed inside. The driver took a step forward and stopped suddenly, eyes going wide before he scrambled for the truck. The truck bounced twice as hard going out, the driver damned near wiping out at the turn that took him out of range of the rifle's sight. The niggling idea that he knew who the driver was made him wish he had Gig, his tech guy, to run facial rec.

The huge door began to swing shut, slowly, proving how heavy it was.

He couldn't get a look at what lay inside, either, which meant more damned recon. He'd have to get up close and personal, which started with freezing up those cameras he could see.

Something was in there, something big, and he was going to have to figure out how to get in. This was not just a search and destroy, it was information gathering on the weapons that had everyone running so fucking scared, including the guy who had just made a drop of some kind of animal.

Whatever the fuck they were. They were obviously biologicals. That was always a goddamn disaster. Living things were uncontrollable as fuck. Look at dudes who made movies with dogs, and that was no comparison to what biologicals could do in wartime. He'd seen this werewolf once who ripped the throat out of two soldiers before turning on his supposed handler, the guy's silver-tipped Taser doing no damned good in the bloodlust.

Mr. Lean and Hairy appeared again, looking up at the sky, muttering to himself, giving Ice a look at a tiny, fine ass. Sweet. At least the scenery would be good.

Something shot across the sky, something akin to a comet. Weird. He would have to check his comms to see if anything was expected in the way of meteor showers. He hadn't seen anything on the recon reports, but intel wasn't always one hundred percent.

The man waved to the sky, grinning up like an idiot, then turned back and hurried inside.

Ice blinked, pulling his long-range binocs out to see if he could get a better glimpse of what was up in the ether. The thing was moving like lightning, flying across the sky like a burning jet. What the fuck? It was no plane, glider, or helicopter.

Nothing he'd ever seen moved that fast. Ever. He gave up trying to figure out what it was and went for deciding where it would land, instead. The trajectory was heading toward the peak of a mountain, then suddenly, it turned left. He watched it plunge downward, then disappear. Damn. He marked the coordinates down.

What the fuck was that? What moved that fast when it was that frickin' big? That had to be some sort of experimental weapon, man.

He started breaking down his little camp. He had to move closer to the hot guy with all the hair. He wanted to know how the hell this whole compound thing worked.

Time to go do his job. Even if it killed him.

Krystal was crying, chuffing out piteously, and Keon padded over to her bed, plopping down beside it. "Oh, baby girl. What's wrong?"

She crawled into his lap, pink scales warm and smooth on his lap. She was surprisingly light for her size, and loneliness poured off her in waves.

"Missing Momma, I bet. It's okay, baby girl." Dragons were incredibly sensitive to change, and Krystal had been through enough for two lifetimes, let alone her short one.

Her momma had been displaced, and there were shockingly few places left for creatures as big as a full-sized dragon. Krystal needed raising, at least until her mom got new digs. Literally. A bunker would have to be excavated.

The wee one, though, was scared and alone, needing support and a little attention. "Don't worry. Tomorrow I'll show you the new baby, and you and Serena and Malachi can play outside."

Nine.

Nine babies under ten.

He was going to lose his shit. That was bad. Dragons needed a stable environment.

Krystal started whimpering again and Keon forced himself to breathe, to let it go. These babies needed him. He reached out to scratch her eye ridges, listening to her noises become a purr almost.

"Such a pretty girl. You'll have to teach the new little one all about being happy."

She blinked at him, so sleepy now that her eyes wouldn't stay open. He sang softly, rocking her, needing her to settle so he could do his evaluation on the new hatchling. That baby boy was the youngest he'd ever had, both parents murdered like beasts, just because some poacher thought he deserved a dragon. Fuck.

And Sergei acting like some bigwig, threatening him. Asshat. He was a Guardian. He didn't deal in human politics. All Sergei had to do was deliver eggs and babies when the man found them.

A deep rumble came from Chi, the yearling who was just learning to cast out with his senses. He chuckled and eased Krystal into her bedding before heading over to his blue boy. Blue. How rare was that? "What's up, baby boy?" He reached out to Chion, too, knowing touch would help.

Chion whimpered and growled, twisting under his hands. *Ice. Ice ice ice.*

"Are you thirsty?"

Chion grumbled and grunted, skin so hot it steamed.

"Poor baby. I'll get you something. Hold on." No fevers. None. Zero.

Visions of icicles slammed into his head.

"Okay. Okay, bath. Let's get in the water, baby." He picked Chi up, heading toward the pool. The silly boy started to struggle, fire building up in that small body. The little guy was never hot like this. Not like so many of the others. "Baby. Baby, easy."

The wee one hit the ground and ran for the window, crying piteously, wings flapping even though he couldn't fly yet -- wings weren't big enough to hold his weight up.

"Shit." He scrambled for the window, trying to figure out what was up. There wasn't anything out there that he could see.

Nothing but trees and sky. The night was clear enough he could see all the way to the ridge.

Chi pushed against the window, crying hard, tiny leather wings beating the glass. A crack appeared, right at the bottom of the lowest pane. "Chi, stop. You'll hurt yourself." He had to get the baby boy to calm down before he went to see what was up. "Did you see something out there?" The icicles came again, sharp and pointed, almost driving him to his knees. "Okay. I'll go look, but you have to stay here. Right here?"

The tiny dragon whined, but sat, tail flicking.

Keon grabbed a baseball bat and headed outside. Guns did funny things around dragons. He checked the perimeter, frowning mightily. No footprints. No sounds. No -- whoa. What was that on the eastern security camera?

He headed over, frowning. *Ice?* Ice, coating the lens of the camera. It was easily sixty degrees out here, even as dark as it was.

Iceiceiceiceice.

Shit. Ice. Now he got it.

He sighed. Just what he needed, a baby dragon imprinting on... someone. Something? Someone was in the compound, and the only way Chi could imprint on them was if they'd been peering in windows, using the cover of those iced-up cameras to sneak around.

"Okay, I know you're out here. What do you want?" It might just shock someone into answering. All he heard was chirping crickets. And a crying dragonet. "I swear to all that is holy, if you hurt him, I'll make you pay. Leave us alone."

He stopped short of shaking his fist at the night, but honestly, this could make his life impossible. Imprinting could be dangerous. Hell, it could kill the dragon if the imprinter refused the connection, and this was obviously someone with less than honest intentions. Hopefully it wasn't Sergei, who'd wanted to trade the new hatchling he'd brought in for an older dragon to take home with him.

Whoever it was, if they refused the connection his sweet boy was going to be inconsolable. Keon sighed. "Look, I have a baby in there who won't stop crying until he sees you. If you're a decent human being, come on and knock on my door. I'm not here to hurt anyone. I'm just a Guardian."

Iceiceice. Ice!

"Not only that, but the headache you have? It won't go away until you do." He turned on his heel and went back inside. He knew whatever happened would have to come in its own time.

Until then, he had a baby boy to comfort and a newborn to deal with.

Damn it.

Chapter Two

I ce has gone AWOL."

"What?" Jacques, also known as One-Eyed Jack, rolled out of his bunk, staring at the team tech guy, Gig. "He said he'd be gon' for a week, debriefin' over the whole Spider incident."

Gig's mouth flattened into a hard line. "Well, he lied."

"How do you know?" Shannon, their big Irish wolfdog of a man, leaned down from the top bunk, staring at Gig intently.

"He's gone off the grid. I can't get him on his phone or email, and his tracker is dead as a doornail."

They all contemplated that in silence. They all had a tracking chip. If Ice's had been deactivated…

"Well, we need to fin' him, 'den." Jacques was acting team leader when Ice was gone, and he was sick of sitting on his ass, pretending Ice hadn't snuck out and left them, just like their team member Damon had. They were not going to lose Ice, too. Even if he wanted to be lost.

Gig nodded. "The last place I saw his signal was somewhere near Portland."

"Good. That gives us a place to start. Ice isn't exactly easy to hide."

Shannon hooted, the sound echoing off the ceiling. "Yeah. He blends."

They all grinned at each other, even Gig breaking a smile.

"Shan, you get to the other building and get the rest of the guys. Gig, get us coordinates. We're getting our guy back, no matter what the Man has him doing."

The guys moved out, and Jacques got his ass moving, packing his gear. Time to go save Ice's miserable ass from whatever he thought he was saving the team from.

Ice counted his pulse behind his eyes. Bang. One. Bang. Two. Ever since he'd managed a glimpse inside the long building at the creatures inside, his head felt like there was a blacksmith in there, banging away with a hammer on an anvil. He had no idea how long it had been going on, but he was pretty sure it had been two full nights without sleep what with travel and all.

It was driving him batty, like a low-grade constant cry, grating at him. He wanted to claw his eyes out and freeze his brain.

Please. Please. Iceiceiceiceice. Please.

"Shut up," he muttered.

The cries got more piteous, loud, kinda like an upset husky dog at three times the volume.

"I know you're out there! He's going to die! Please, whoever you are." It was Mr. Hair, standing at the door, a pale blue creature in his arms.

Die? Why would some weird lizard die because of him? Ice grunted, the pain in his head driving him to his knees. Okay. Maybe how didn't matter. He began crawling because he couldn't stand. He'd go see what was what, because if he didn't, his head would explode.

Iceiceiceiceiceice! Ice! Ice! The dude brought the little blue thing over and it wrapped around him, the headache disappearing so fast it made him nauseated. He dry-heaved a little, his belly quaking. Christ, this was definitely a weapon if it could incapacitate him like this. Cold sweat beaded up even as he stroked the little monster perched on his chest. Waves of sensation poured over him, the little thing near hysterical with relief.

The other guy hummed, though. "See, Chi? See? He's here. You're okay."

"Gonna puke, man." Not only had he blown his cover and his advantage, he was on the ground about to lose his guts. He was a professional.

"Breathe. Breathe. It'll ease, I promise."

"If you say so, man." This guy wasn't trying to bash his head in, at least.

"Just breathe. Chi, I'm going to get him some water, okay? You be good."

Ice would be damned but the lizard nodded. Then nuzzled up under his chin with a surprisingly not slimy head and trilled happily. He'd gone to la-la land.

A glass of water pushed into his hand and he drank deep, the cold water filling him up. Better. Much better. He snorted, feeling like a fool. "So, these are the big scary weapons and you're a criminal mastermind. My ass."

"Huh? You're sitting on your backside. I can't see if it's a weapon."

"It can be if Gig is making the chili." He sighed, patting the weird animal hanging from his neck when it sighed, too. "You got any more water?"

"I do." His glass was taken from him. "Would you like to come in?"

Uh-huh. Criminal fucking genius, this guy, handing him a lizard and inviting him in. "Sure. Why not." He'd have tea and crumpets or something. What the fuck was a crumpet, anyway?

"Chi, you want to come with me?"

Iceiceiceiceiceiceice. The sensation was like being hugged tight, the sounds echoing in his head. Ow. And also whoa.

"Okay, but be a good boy."

"He's not heavy."

"Not yet. Give him ten years."

Ice tried to look at the little thing. "Uh… what is it?"

"What is what?"

He was led into a… whoa. Jesus. This was a cavern, a huge, warm, well-lit cavern.

"This?" He touched the little guy again, the wee animal.

"Him. His name is Chi."

"Why is he all over me?" Surreal. This was just bizarre, and he thought he was pretty used to that.

"He imprinted on you when you were snooping."

"What?" Was that English?

"You had to be peering in the windows and he made eye contact. It happens." So matter-of-fact. A giant lizard looked at you and boom, it was in your goddamn brain. Faboo.

The little guy around his neck made a distressed noise, and Ice winced at the pain in his head. *Okay. It's okay.*

Ice. A soft purr filled the air.

The screw drilling into his skull eased off. Woo. He kept petting, fingers stroking the warm, fascinating scales. The little guy was surprisingly warm against Ice's always cold skin.

The human guy wandered off into the shadows, every so often murmuring to someone, humming softly. Ice could only imagine what he was talking to. There was really nowhere to sit, so he stood there, feeling like an idiot.

Soft snoring filled the air, Chi going lax in his arms. He tiptoed around after that, poking his nose where it didn't belong, he'd bet. Still, this was recon, so he might as well make the best of it.

The place was huge, with dozens of giant crates filled with soft blankets, as well as hallways that led off in all directions, carved right into the rock around them.

"So what is it you do here?" He hoped Mr. Naked was still around.

"I live here. My family has owned this land for generations."

That was no answer. When he stepped closer to the voice he could hear, a bass rumble he couldn't identify had him stepping back.

"Damien really would prefer that you ask to come back in his lair."

"Who's Damien?" That couldn't be a man back there. Of

course, it could be a shifter, maybe. Spider had hooked up with two of those, a wolf and a cat.

"My bonded. He's shy and he says you're military and here to hurt the babies."

"Your what?" Maybe his head hurt because he'd hit it.

"My bonded. Are you hungry? I need to start some food. I'm starving."

"Who are you?"

"Keon. Who are you?"

"Ice." It seemed silly to try to lie after the whole head explosion thing. And it told this guy just as much as he'd told Ice.

"Ah. That explains a lot. Do you eat dairy? I have cheese."

"I do." He'd eat his damned MREs if he could get to them right now.

"Cool." A light came on, a remarkably normal-looking kitchen illuminated. "I've already fed everyone else."

"How many is everyone?" He was starting to think this was a suicide mission for sure. Only he'd end up killing himself because he'd lost his mind.

"I probably shouldn't say." A pot of something was pulled out of the fridge. "It's my job to protect them."

"Look, man, I don't think you're dangerous." Ice waved a hand. "So I got to tell you, someone thinks you're planning a coup."

"A coup? Like a takeover? I haven't been to a town with more than one hundred and fifty people in eight years."

"You look like it." It slipped out, but dude, the guy looked like a wild man. A hot one, with a sharp, hawk nose and deeply tanned skin, a lot of which was on display. Ice liked. He liked the friendly smile and the almost black eyes, too.

"There's not much need for formality around here." Bread and cheese landed on the counter, along with a long, wickedly sharp knife. "Who sent you, exactly?"

"I'm just on recon." That was a flat-out lie, and a non-answer of his own.

"Huh. Recon." Keon didn't sound convinced.

"Yep. Identify the target." Soft snores under his chin made him chuckle.

He had to admit, this little thing was adorable. Pale blue and shiny, pointed muzzle and huge bright eyes.

"I have no intention of making this place a target." This time the words were serious, soft, without a hint of fear.

"Well, someone has that intention, man."

"Then they're fools." The knife sliced through the cheese. *Thwack.*

"Tell me why. I can help." Or at least not get himself killed

"This is a rescue. That's what I do. Keep the little ones safe."

Talking to this man was like swimming in circles in a vortex.

A plate was brought to him and the tiny beast was taken, a soft crying starting in his head immediately. His temples throbbed in time. "He can stay with me if he wants."

"He wants."

Chi came back to him, settling close, still sound asleep. How the hell was he gonna handle this when he left?

"He'll steal your cheese if you let him."

Ice snorted. "He's sound asleep."

"They're tricky, the babies. They can surprise you."

"Baby whats?" He'd never seen anything like these creatures.

"Dragons. He's right there, in your lap. Isn't it obvious?"

"Dragons." Ice looked at the wee beast he held. Well, he could hardly not believe in dragons if he believed in himself, or his crew, or any of the other weird things he'd seen. "Huh."

"Uh-huh. Chi is rare. I don't usually see blue ones."

"He's cute." Cute. Dragon. It was like a kid's movie.

"They grow out of it." A deep snarl filled the air and Keon cackled happily. "Most of them."

Okay, that was not a cute sound. That was an I-can-eat-you sound.

"What the fuck is that?"

"Who."

Ice made a frustrated noise. "Okay, who?"

"His name is Damien. He's been with me since I was born."

"Dragons live a long time?" He was trying to get his bearings. Maybe food -- "My cheese is gone."

"I warned you. He likes cheese."

Ice hadn't seen the silly thing move. Laughter rang in his head, clear and bright. "Oh, you're wicked." Patently fake snoring filled the air. He reached under the little guy's chin and scritched. Thin, leathery wings flapped, the snoring turning to a happy purr. Little thief. Ice was only gonna be pissed if there was no more cheese.

Another handful of cheese dropped in the bowl. "Are you interested in chili?"

"Sure." His belly rumbled. "I can offer, uh, apple crisp MRE."

"Uh, no. We'll just have cake after."

"Thanks. I'm so sick of those things." He studied Keon, trying to figure out what made the guy tick.

"There's cornbread and chili first. It's warmish."

"I love heat." He was always freezing, after all.

"Oh, excellent. I use a lot of chilies." Two huge bowls of soup were served up, topped with onions and cheese, then the cornbread was on plates. How domestic. Damned near Texan, like Spider. Man, he was really on the Spider thing. Ice needed to let it go.

"I bet you don't get a lot of company." He caught Chi this time before the little bugger ate all his cheese.

"No. Only new babies and getting them back to families when I can."

"Does he have a family?" Ice patted Chi's head.

"No. Mercs took them both. He's been with me since before he had scales." Keon sat cross-legged in front of him, which was distracting as hell. If he wasn't so hungry, he'd have taken more of the view in.

The chili was hot as hell, warming him deep, and the

cornbread was fresh and buttery. He let himself wallow in the food a little bit, filling his belly. It had been a long time since he'd had anything but military chow or cheap and greasy take-out. This was all vegetables, rich and thick. He didn't know what the fuck to make of this guy. Maybe origami. The idea of folding Keon like a paper crane made him snort happily.

"Good chili?"

A soft crying keen came from another room and Keon sighed, stood. "Please don't try to take him past the main doors. Damien would be put out. Kryssie, I'm coming."

He watched Keon disappear into the shadows of the huge space, then dug Chi's head out of his chili. "That's mine, buddy. How the heck did I get bonded to a dragon?"

Chi chirruped happily, wings fluttering. *Ice.*

"Silly thing." He munched his cornbread.

Silly thing. One claw touched his chest.

Ice chuckled, staring down into the beast's jewel-like eyes.

Ice. Good Ice. Bite? Cheese? The voice was so, so clear. It rang in his head, but it didn't hurt like this when Chi was happy.

"Just don't make yourself sick, kiddo." He gave Chi another bite of cheese. Images and words flashed through his head, wild and bright and shiny. He shook his head, his ears ringing a little. "Whoa."

"It'll ease. Just remember to breathe."

"I'm trying. Dude, who are you? How do you do this?"

"My family have been guardians for generations. I can't imagine not hearing them. I'd be lost." Keon sat in front of him and grabbed his head, eyes going wide. "You're cold! Chi! You found someone else blue, you clever baby!"

Ice blinked into Keon's dark eyes, feeling like someone else had just hijacked his brain. Chi had been one thing, but he felt this bizarre connection to Keon, too.

"Oh. Oh. You're okay. You're okay."

"Am I? I feel weird." This day was just getting more bizarre by the moment.

"It's just new. Remember to breathe."

"Breathe?" First a dragon baby, and now this guy. Ice wanted to run in circles and scream. Some professional soldier he was.

"Mm-hmm. In and out. Over and over. It makes it easier."

Iceiceice. The little dragon climbed up on his shoulder, breathing in his ear like a steam locomotive.

"Be gentle, Chi. He's brand new."

Breathebreathebreathe.

Ice sucked in a breath, bonding with the dragon easier than the man. Tiny, sharp claws combed through his hair, grooming him. "Is this normal?"

"Grooming? He's trying to comfort you."

"My head is gonna explode." Ice felt a little lightheaded, in fact. More floaty than 'splodey.

"Come stretch out. I'll make you a nest."

"A nest?" He blinked again, feeling like he was gonna just fall over.

"Uh-huh. Pillows, blankets. Comfy things. You can stay in Chi's room."

Somehow he was up and walking, led to a tiny room with a pile of blankets on a hammock. He was pushed in, Chi on his chest, and someone took his boots off, covered him up.

He curled up with the wee dragon, a feeling of peace settling over him.

He couldn't sleep in here like this. He couldn't.

He…

Keon headed to his room. Damien's huge head rested in the doorway, bright emerald eyes gleaming.

"He's sleeping. That baby totally imprinted on him." Keon stepped into his room, stopping to caress the spiky faux horns on Damien's forehead.

Damien rumbled, the sound accompanied by a curl of smoke.

"I know, dearest, but what was I supposed to do?" He settled on the floor by Damien's neck.

Damien rumbled again, and he saw an image in his head of a very singed military guy. *Whoosh.*

"Yeah, but what about Chi?" He hated losing a kit, especially if he could help it, and Ice seemed perfectly honorable.

Damien sighed, the sound gusty.

"I know. I'm dealing with it. I promise."

Keeeeeon.

Damien's mental happy sound made Keon smile.

He leaned in, nuzzling the warm, smooth scales. *Dearest one.*

HappyChi. HappyHappy. Damien would know if the little beast was happy. All dragons heard each other.

"That's right. Happy happy." Damien shifted, the floor seeming to creak. "Does someone need a belly scritch?"

Scritchscritchscritch.

Yeah, someone had some itchy scales. "Well, turn over a little, you amazing beast." Keon had to smile, he had to. Damien was pure joy.

One clawed foot lifted, and Damien rolled to his side, giving Keon those big belly armor pieces. Oh, his sweet dragon. He scratched, and Damien began to purr for him, the sound more familiar than his own breath. He couldn't remember a time without his dragon. He couldn't imagine a life alone.

Oh, he hoped this Ice guy wasn't an asshole. Chi would just die of a broken heart. Maybe dragons didn't bond with assholes.

Damien snorted smoke.

"A guy can hope, right?"

He could hear Chi murmuring happily in his sleep, all about ice and snow and brrrsoftfurry. The others started dreaming too, purring and growling together, and Keon smiled. They were all connected. No wonder the ice-man's head hurt.

Scratching, most loved.

"Sorry, Damien." He had a very important job to do.

My keeper. Mine.

"Possessive butthead."

Damien's laughter filled his head, ringing inside him. Yeah, dragons were something else. Good thing Keon liked them.

Chapter Three

Ice woke up feeling almost warm. That was an amazing thing that hadn't happened since that one time he and Spider had torn each other up after a near death experience.

Iceiceice. Spiders?

Ice brought to mind what his former teammate Damon looked like, figuring the little dragon would get the idea.

The question eased and then the little critter stretched, muscles rippling. Then the oddest barking-chirrupping sound filled the room, and it was echoed by more of the same sounds from outside his chamber.

Ice heard a husky laugh. "Then come and eat, babies. Oatmeal and fruit salad today."

"They eat oatmeal?" He unwrapped Chi's tail from his neck to keep from choking.

"Don't you?"

Oatmeal! Apples. Oranges. Grapes.

Ice clutched his head, the noise in there rising to an alarming level.

"Easy. Try to hum a little, see if that doesn't help. Something to blanket it. Chi, baby, make the others quiet inside him, yeah? You have to take care of your Keeper."

Chi blinked at him, and damned if his head didn't ease off. Oh, man.

"Good baby! So good." Keon came in, wearing a pair of loose, soft, so-thin-they-were-nearly-see-through pants.

Ice's body surprised him by tightening, his cock rising some. "Do you ever wear clothes?"

"I'm always burning up. It's a thing." Keon offered him a grin and a cup of coffee. "Good morning."

"This place is kind of like a heat rock." Oh, God. Coffee. Good coffee. Really good, rich, not-instant coffee. Ice breathed deep, the aroma perking him up.

"There's oatmeal for us too, if you're hungry."

"Starving." He stretched, starting to feel way more human. *Starving. Oats. Ice. Apples.*

Keon chuckled. "They love apples."

"No kidding." He chuckled. "Do you have a necessary or do I need to go outside?"

"Oh, we're equipped. Come, I'll show you."

How big was this place, anyway? Ice heard echoes that sounded like a furnace banging to life, and the sound seemed huge. He was led down one hewn stone hallway after another, deeper into the mountain. Finally it opened up into a bathing chamber that...

Christ.

There had to be a toilet. He hoped.

"The water closet is behind the screen. There are cleaning tubs and then the big pool is for relaxing. Towels are in the closets. The big pool is heated."

"Wow. I'll revisit this for sure." After he peed. And had oatmeal.

"If you can't find your way back, call for Chi. He'll get you." The little dragon fluttered to the floor and skittered off, muttering about oats and apples.

"Thanks." Dragons were hungry. Like all the time. Constantly. Always. Ice guessed it took a lot to keep the little critters going. He made sure he was alone before he hit the head. He didn't figure that was something he wanted to share.

The noise from the other rooms was amazing, Keon laughing and clanging pots, singing happily. God, this couldn't be real. Maybe he'd fallen and hit his head. He washed up, and pondered changing into his extra kit, but those clothes were dirty, too.

He walked out, blinking as a pile of clean clothes were there, his blue Chi atop them. *Tada!*

"Wow, you got me clothes. What a good dragon." Did he just say that?

Chi fluttered, bowed and bobbed. *Good. Good me.* A pair of socks were snapped up, offered over. *Feet clothes.*

He grabbed them, grinning. Feet clothes. Okay, he was totally besotted with this little guy.

Chi jabbered at him, the action more concepts than words, and it didn't hurt today. It was more joy bouncing in his head, making him grin. The clothes were… kinda skimpy. He'd work with them, but he'd freeze if he had to go outside.

Chi gathered his other clothes, stumbling away. *Keon! Stinky Ice clothes!*

Nice to know the little guy thought he smelled. He headed out of the bathing room, stopping short when he almost tripped over the biggest tail he'd ever seen.

"Holy shit."

No. Serena. Chi's voice was sure, happy. *Serena. Ice.*

"Serena." This was what Chi was going to grow into?

The tail slid and then disappeared, a beautiful pair of topaz eyes blinking at him out of a long, slender face. God, how beautiful. She was a pretty girl, for sure. Lovely, with reddish-orange scales, she slid past him into the bathing room, managing to look sleek for all her bulk.

"Serena, can Daisy and Blaze come with you, please?"

How many were there?

"Do you need some help, man?"

"Come have breakfast."

Two dragons barreled down the hallway together, claws clacking as they headed for the water. Ice slid out of the way, then followed the sound of Keon's voice and Chi's chittering. "Is Chi gonna get that big?"

"How big?"

"As big as Serena." The oatmeal suddenly smelled amazing.

Keon snorted. "Oh, she's still an adolescent. She's about half her full size, and she's a female…"

There was more coffee, toast, fruit salad and… He stopped, blinked. There were at least a dozen more eating, some twice Chi's size. One was in Keon's hand, eating tiny bites of banana, looking almost like a toy. "Half her size." He just munched, needing to keep his mouth busy.

"Yep." Keon didn't look worried.

"Lord." Weapons. Christ. The higher-ups had no fucking idea.

"Do you want toast?" The little one in Keon's hand was sound asleep, curled in a tiny ball.

"Yeah. Starving."

The baby, because that had to be what she was, was put in a tiny padded box, blanket covering her. "She gets cold."

"She's so little." Ice knew somehow he'd been transported to another dimension, so he might as well go for it.

"She's just hatched. She'll grow. This is the hard part, you know? They deserve their parents. I'm a pale substitute."

That odd, deep growl sounded again, filling the air. "Is someone about to eat me?"

Keon laughed, the sound ringing out. "That was for me. He doesn't like it if I run myself down."

"Who?" He glanced around, looking for the source of the noise.

"Damien. My bonded."

"So, uh." Ice stuffed toast in his mouth before he asked anything more horrifying.

"It's a lot to take in, huh?"

"It is. And I know from weird." Ice was the least of his team sometimes, when it came to talent.

"They're important. Special. I'll protect them from anything."

"I'm not here to hurt them." He had been. Now he had to figure out how to let his team know his assignment had gone tits up.

"Good. You're too hot to burn to a crisp."

"Fire elemental tried that once. It didn't work."

"I bet dragons are harder."

"To survive, you mean?" Maybe. They were bigger than Spider, for sure.

"Yeah." Keon started picking up bowls and separating dragons that were starting to snarl over food. Suddenly Ice noticed how tired Keon looked, how worn.

He wasn't one for altruism, but he wanted to reach out, ask Keon if he needed help. Anything. So he did. "What can I do?"

"Do? I… I don't know."

"I can help." He wolfed down two pieces of toast and fed one to Chi. "Really."

"Maggie and Marvin, the twins. They fight over everything."

"Ah. So you need to feed one and I'll feed the other." He could just give one a shot of chill if it got toothy.

"Oh, that would be nice." The little beasts were at it again.

"Here, I'll take this one." He took the red boy on the left.

"Maggie, if you bite at him one more time."

"Come on, buddy. Over here." Ice put fruit out for the little dragon, pulling Chi away from it.

Chi chirruped softly, grumping when that didn't get him more apples.

Keon worked hard, picking dishes up, putting refilled ones down, comforting and singing and petting.

It was a frigging daycare in here. A lizard daycare. Ice shook his head, then yelped. "Chi. No biting."

Not a lee-zurd.

No? He tried not talking out loud. *You look like one.*

Do not! I look like wyvern. The little voice got softer. *Keon say blue is pretty.*

Oh, it must be hard, being the only blue dragon. He got that. Ice had never met anyone else who had his talent. Ice nodded, reaching down to scoop up his baby dragon. "Blue is the best."

Blue is the best. Those tiny wings fluttered madly.

"Yep. My blue Chi." God that was adorable.

The wee thing offered the older red male a grape. That worked, the red male dragon munching happily.

"Thank you for your help." Keon smiled at him, up to his elbows in soapy water.

That smile made a ball of warmth bloom in his icy belly. Weird.

Keon's nostrils flared, and that warmth grew into heat. He stared, the mostly naked form looking downright edible. Man, it had been too long if this was getting to him so fast. Right? If it had been too long for him, how long had it been for Keon? Now, that was a thought worth pondering.

"I…" Keon stepped back, his hand covering a raging hard-on. "Can you keep an eye on them?"

"Uh." Ice moved, following Keon's retreat. "No? I think you need a hand more than they do."

"Oh, it's not--" Those eyes were like flames, and another big dragon passed by, Chi going to her easily.

"Hey, I can help with that, too." He so could. In fact, he was far more expert at sex than he was at feeding dragons.

"Can you?" Keon kept moving, the hallways obviously empty. Smart little critters.

"Uh-huh. I like it, even. I like the looks of what you're hiding."

"I'm… No one comes up here for that."

Oh, man, that sucked. "Well, I didn't come for that originally, but I'm sure here now." He had no idea what had come over him, but he wanted Keon. Immediately. He wanted to see that long pretty prick, wanted to touch it. Wanted that mouth on him. His balls pulled up a little at the thought, making him grunt.

Keon's nostrils flared again and Ice could swear he felt heat pouring from that lean body. It drew him like a proverbial moth to flame. He needed that warmth. Keon's back hit a wall, and Ice stopped, a heartbeat from contact.

"Tell me no one will fry me for this." Ice reached out and touched Keon's cheek.

"No one will fry…" Keon leaned into his touch, lips parting.

"Oh, good." He tugged Keon to him, closing the last few inches between them to take that pretty mouth with his lips. The connection between them flared, sharp and electric, hot as flame. The kiss made him moan, made his body come to life.

Keon made the best sound, wild and rough, needy.

They rocked together a little, their bodies rubbing, their cocks pushing through clothes. Keon was a flame, opening up, tongue sliding on his. Ice grabbed that fine ass, the thin pants no barrier. Oh, fucking A. Feel that -- tight and hard, a perfect double handful. He squeezed, thinking of how hot Keon would be inside.

He rubbed them together, over and over, the friction damn near perfect. He wanted just a little more skin, a little more touch. Keon's hands moved over his chest, over his nipples, down his belly. Ice sucked in a deep breath, his muscles quivering.

"Tingles." Keon had that right; every touch was like a spark of electricity on his skin.

"As long as it doesn't tickle, man." He smiled, licking his lips, then Keon's.

"Not into that." Keon pushed their lips together, tongue fucking his mouth.

He would have nodded if he could. Ice held on instead, kissing Keon back, hard and deep. Sweet, the man's mouth was fucking sweet as honey. Hotter than a two-dollar pistol, too, sending warmth to Ice's toes.

Keon's hands wrapped around his head, tilting him so their kiss could go on and on. Ice hummed, sliding one hand around to slip it down Keon's pants. Oh, fine, long prick. Keon was hard as diamonds, the tip dripping with need.

Perfect. Ice licked his lips again, debating.

"What? You don't want to?"

"Huh? I was trying to decide whether to suck you or fuck you, man."

"Oh, God." Keon shuddered, shook against him. "Can I have both?"

He felt a slow smile dawn on his face. "Oh, yeah." He dropped to his knees, yanking Keon's pants down. Oh, look at that... Smooth and hairless, a long fine cock crowned with ink, a sinuous, traveling pattern that looked almost like words. A little spurt of jealousy slid through him, surprise stinging his nerves. "Who did this?"

"The couple I replaced. They did it to celebrate my calling. They weren't related, so it wasn't weird."

"Oh." Well, he guessed that was okay. This was less celebrating calling, more getting it on. He leaned over and licked, tasting.

He leaned back, shocked. It tingled.

Tingled. Okay, that was hot. Literally. If he didn't have ice water in his veins, it might have burned him.

"I can't stop it. I'm sorry." Keon stared down at him as if waiting for him to run.

"It's fucking amazing." He licked again, then sucked the head between his lips.

"Oh, fuck..." Ice heard the clunk of Keon's head against the wall, dull and distant.

Yeah. Oh, hell yes. Keon's flavor was like all the hot things: spices, a slow-burning fire, peppers that ranked high on the Scoville scale. He'd thought he'd felt heat before. No fucking way. This man was on fire for him, and he sucked all the way down to the root.

Gentle hands tangled in his short hair, tugging him. "Please. Please, man. Don't stop."

Nope. No stopping. He licked and sucked, closing his eyes to feel and smell and taste. It was just like eating Red Hots -- every liquid drop made him need another one to keep the burn at a reasonable level.

Ice swallowed, letting the top of Keon's cock hit the roof of his mouth. The lean muscles of Keon's legs jumped and jerked under his hands. He loved that, loved the way Keon's balls drew up. Somebody was needing it, wanting attention. Maybe craving it so hard he'd called Ice there. That might explain a lot, actually.

Keon rocked, pressed deep, and called out for him.

He squeezed those fine ass cheeks. Sucking, hollowing his cheeks. Hot as fire, with such smooth skin. God.

"Close. I'm close. Oh, fuck…"

When Keon spilled between his lips, it burned all the way down his throat, like he'd swallowed too-hot coffee. It was perfect, making him moan, his hips humping the air. As soon as his mouth popped off that heavy cock, Keon pushed him over, that blistering mouth covering his prick.

He pushed his fingers into Keon's wild hair, feeling it like a live thing, curling up around his wrists. "Thought you wanted me to fuck you, man."

"Yes. Slicking you up." That hot tongue slid along his shaft.

"Oh. Oh, damn. Uh…" He hated to ruin the mood, but most guys wanted a rubber.

"Don't be silly. We're not human, not purely, hmm?"

"No. No, but most of the guys I've been with worried." He grinned down at Keon's bent head. Bareback. Fucking A. He hadn't managed that, ever.

"I'm not." Hot lips covered him again, sweet and fierce all at once.

He could get used to this closeness, the touch of this man. Only this man. Dangerous. Seriously dangerous. Fuck, it was erotic as anything. Keon's fingers cupped his balls, rolled them playfully. He grunted, his toes trying to curl. His skin felt electrified, the tingles constant now.

Keon's head lifted, mouth popping off. "You ready?"

"Fuck, yes. You need a little help, though." He licked his fingers, got them good and wet. It didn't take a second for Keon to slide up along his body, touch every inch of him. He pushed his hand behind the man, letting two slick fingers ease inside Keon's body. Whoa, tight. "You ever done this before?"

"Long time ago."

"We'll get you nice and open, then." Ice wanted this to be good. Really good, so Keon would want to do it over and over. That tiny little hole gripped his fingers, held him tight. He concentrated on keeping his motions steady, working his fingers in, then out, Keon on fire inside. Keon didn't seem worried or tense, the man relaxed against him, riding him like a natural.

They fit together so well this way that Ice figured he was gonna explode when he got his cock inside Keon. Boom. Of course, his spunk was cold. Most guys freaked after that. No telling what Keon would think.

Hopefully freaking out was not on the menu. He grinned a little. With no condom, he might-ought to warn the man.

Or not.

Maybe it was tacky, but he liked the honest response. He pushed a little deeper, his fingertips sliding over the sweet spot he knew he'd find right there.

"Oh. Oh, sweet fuck." Keon's eyes went wide, almost shocked. "Ice."

"Uh-huh. Feel that? Wait until I get my cock in you and hit it until you scream for me."

"Sounds like the best plan ever." Keon twisted, body sliding along his, every contact like a little static shock.

Oh, fuck, that eager joy just did it for him, one hundred percent. He grunted, unable to wait any longer. He had to get inside Keon now. Ice tugged his fingers free, sliding in between Keon's thighs.

Keon didn't tense, spread for him easily, let him at that tiny hole. Ice went as slowly as he could, the head of his cock popping through the tight ring of muscle, making them both moan. He could feel the fluttering of Keon's muscles, butterfly wings against him.

Maybe something bigger.

God. He pushed harder, seating himself all the way in.

Keon lifted up onto his elbows, dark eyes huge. "So full."

"You're tight, baby." The pet name popped out, but Keon didn't seem to mind.

He pulled back, Keon's body dragging on his shaft. The

friction made him grit his teeth, his hips jerking. He needed to move faster, the heat building until it was an amazing mix of pain and pleasure.

"More. More. I feel you everywhere."

"I'm inside you." He looked into Keon's dark eyes, completely unable to believe this was happening so damned fast, so intense. This was no zipless fuck. This had already earned a repeat.

"Yes." Keon reached up, hand leaving a trail of fire behind it on his belly, his chest.

His nipples were so tight they might jump off his chest, and he shivered, goose bumps rising. How could he be so hot and have chills? This was fucking amazing.

"It's good?" Keon pinched his nipples, tugged.

"Better than that." Words failed how hot this was.

"Excellent." Keon worked him like a guitar player, fingers never clumsy, even as he plowed that tight little hole.

He was the one who felt breathless and clumsy, like this was the first time, like he was completely untried. Keon's face was a study in need, hungry and focused on him. Maybe he wasn't fumbling the ball too damned bad, then.

He bent for a kiss, needing to break the intensity of their stare. Their mouths met and he felt Keon's response all around his cock. Tightening down, Keon squeezed, and Ice grunted, his breath huffing in his chest. He dragged one of his hands down Keon's body, settling to cup Keon's hot little ass and pull them closer together. Then he rocked his hips, looking for that angle. He'd promised screaming.

"Please." The word was whispered into his lips. "Oh, fuck. Please."

"I got you." He did. He just needed to slide up -- There. Bang. The tip of his cock connected with that tiny gland.

Keon sucked in a sharp, deep breath, eyes wide as saucers. Bingo.

"There it is." Sucking air, Ice started moving again, hitting that spot over and over.

The fine son of a bitch went wild underneath him, giving it up and letting him see how good it was. He grinned, feeling a little studly. A lot. Whatever. His cock was in the tightest, hottest place he'd ever been in, and Ice thought he might be the one to end up screaming.

A low string of words that weren't anything he understood flew from Keon's lips and then the man reached for that long, slender prick, jacking it.

"Uh-huh. Show me, baby. Let me see you come."

"Oh, heavens." The words sounded shocked, almost prim, Keon's expression pure surprise.

"Now, Keon." He needed to feel it around him, that orgasm.

"Now. Now." Keon cupped his cheek, and he jerked at the heat.

He nodded, his cock so hard he might explode. He came, and Keon went over the edge with him, both of them shuddering and crying out.

"Oh, fuck. So fucking good." Keon's head rocked from side to side, throat working. "Feel you. So deep."

Not cold. Deep. It was like Keon hadn't even noticed how cold his spunk felt.

Wow. That was -- damn. Ice listened to his heart pound in time with Keon's and knew this had been a suicide mission of sorts. He was never going to be able to go back to his old life.

Keon drew him in, kissed him, tongue fucking his lips with a lazy rhythm.

Ice opened up for the kiss, hearing cheering dragons somewhere in the back of his mind. Somehow the prospect of hanging around here with Keon didn't bother him at all.

"You got a bead on Ice?" Jacques sipped subpar coffee from a military issue cup and watched Chino, their radio and surveillance guy, step back from the long-range lens he'd set up on the side of the ridge. Fuck, the mountains made for interesting times, even if it was weirdly warm for this part of the world.

"I do. He's in the compound down there. We have a bit of an issue, though."

"What's 'dat?"

"We're not the only ones watching. There's a group on the other side of the ridge. They're trying not to be too obvious, but it's tough to cover that many paramilitary types."

"Show me." He had no idea why Ice had broken recon and cover and all the other rules of engagement to go into the compound they'd been surveilling, but they could work that out later. For now, he needed to know who else was taking an interest in the weird mine-like entrance to the semi-active volcanic mountain they perched on.

Chino showed him the image on the scope. Yeah, twenty or more guys milling around a command tent and a couple of troop movers. Not exactly trying keeping out of sight, were they? So obviously Ice wasn't in a military compound or anything. This had to be a private contractor.

"What the hell you gon' and got yourself into, Ice?" Jacques murmured. "They fixing to attack you and you jus' sittin'."

"The whole thing is making my teeth itch," Gig murmured.

The whole team groaned. Gig's itches were always bad.

"Who wants to volunteer for close-up recon?" Jacques knew they had to get a better look at both the other team in the vicinity, and the hole Ice had disappeared into.

"I'm on it." Shannon loaded up a pair of handguns and a belt knife. "I'll be on the QT, so if you need me, send a clicker message, not a voice."

"Got it." He had no idea what Ice had gotten into, but they were a team. Whatever it was, they were damned well going to help Ice get out of it.

Chapter Four

*Y*ou*'ve been naughty.*

"Shut up."

Wicked.

"Damien."

A bad, bad man.

"Stop it or I'll feed you rotten bananas for a week."

His dragon snorted, puffs of smoke escaping. Keon could hear the laughter there, the amusement at his human frailty.

"He's hot, except he's not, he's cold and I don't burn him, just like you don't burn me and Chi likes him and…" He stopped, glaring at his dragon. "Don't laugh at me!"

I like him. He helps feed the twins.

"Me too." Keon really did, which was crazy, but his job was to protect the babies and Ice didn't twig him at all. They were in no danger from the man. In fact, he thought Ice might have been brought there by the universe to help protect them all. "I want you to meet him."

Bring him to me? Damien had a hard time in the caverns, moving around.

"Of course." He stroked Damien's face, petting gently, stroking the smooth scales. "Now?"

Now is good. Damien's tail snaked around to his ankles, warm and heavy.

"Yeah, the babies are all sleeping."

Go and get him.

"Bossy old man." He headed out to the central room, where

Ice was sitting and staring at the piles of dragons, napping together, tails twined as they dozed.

"Hey. Everything okay?" Ice smiled for him, eyes like chips of ice. The man was beautiful, all pale skin and icy-blond hair, those eyes an intense gray/blue.

"Damien wants to meet you." His cock twitched a little at the look in those eyes. There was nothing cold about that expression.

"Damien is your dragon, right?"

"My bonded, yeah. He's amazing."

"Well, I'm all for it." That smile widened, and Ice looked downright approachable.

"He's waiting." He led Ice back to Damien's place, his beautiful dragon waiting. "He's bigger than you might think. He's an adult. He waited for me for a long, long time."

"Is it rude to ask how old he is?" Ice followed slowly, but he didn't sound worried, just curious.

"Almost three hundred years old. A fully grown male." And he'd waited for Keon for one hundred and fifty of those.

"Wow." Ice touched his back, fingers brushing lightly. "That's a long time."

"It is. Time is different in their eyes."

"Is it?" Ice sniffed, and Keon knew the scent of Damien lay heavy in the cavern.

"Dearest? I brought Ice to meet you. Come say hello?" The sound of scale on stone sounded, Damien's big head appearing in the opening to his sleeping chamber.

Keon smiled, stepped forward to touch Damien's scales. "Damien, Ice. Ice, Damien."

"Wow." Ice studied Damien, smiling. "You're amazing."

Damien purred, preened a bit. *I like him.*

"You're a slut," he teased. "An amazing slut."

"May I give him a scratching? Chi seems to like that." Ice had the best instincts for the dragons, polite, yet interested.

Scritch. Scriiiiiitch.

"He would love that."

"Awesome. Tell me if I'm being rude?" Ice stepped in and went right for the heavy ridges over Damien's eyes. That was one of the places such a big animal could never reach.

Damien purred, eyes closing. *My neck, keeper. Scratch my neck.*

"Spoiled dragon." He moved to scratch those bigger scales.

"He's itchy. Do you, uh, moisturize?"

"When he bathes, I scrub him. He's large enough that it's hard for him." Damien protected the babies, just as he nurtured them.

"I bet. Do you fly?" Oh, look at Ice, figuring out to address Damien directly.

Fly. I soar.

Ice gasped and Keon grinned. Damien couldn't speak to Ice, but they all could project images and emotions. Ice had gotten the same one Keon had, no doubt, of Damien bursting up out of the caves and shooting into the sky, a rocket flying high.

"You're stunning, dearest. Absolutely amazing." Keon leaned, resting hard into his dragon, the *thump thump* of the huge heart like a drum.

Thank you, keeper. He likes you.

Keon hoped so. He genuinely hoped so. Ice was like no one he'd ever met, someone who could take his heat. "He's beautiful, isn't he?" Keon asked.

"Yes. Really. Is this what Chi will grow toward?"

"He will. We lose a number of them in adolescence if they don't bond, but Chi found you already."

"Seriously? They have to bond to live?" Ice stared at Damien, then him. "How do you -- I mean, how do they get the chance?"

"They go out on their own if they don't have parents to raise them."

"That sucks." Ice grimaced. "Even I have a team."

"They have me, but..." He shrugged. He was one man, one soul, and he could support the weight of the younglings, but the adults? He wasn't that big inside.

"You need help."

"I do my best." He really did. Only one man, right? There was so much --

"Oh, hey, I'm not down on you." Ice moved around Damien's cheek to put a hand on his arm. "I just mean you need some free time, you know? Someone to take some of the work on."

Ice's touch cooled the shame, made him moan under his breath.

"That's it, babe. I didn't mean anything bad."

He stepped closer, Damien backing away so that they could move closer to one another. Ice grabbed him and kissed him.

Oh.

Oh, yay.

Also, yum.

The kiss took his breath, Ice holding him hard against that muscled body. His fingers danced over Ice, pushing at clothes, needing skin.

"God, I love your hands." Ice struggled with him, getting their pants off.

"Want you again. You settle me." It was crazy.

"I know." Ice licked a line along his jaw.

He shivered, a chill sliding over his skin, the feeling amazing. The sting when Ice bit his lower lip was warm, though, making his body tingle. Everything inside him was fascinated, addicted to the touches.

He wanted more, wanted to climb Ice's big body and hump.

One of those hands wrapped around his ass, fingertips digging in. Ice held him effortlessly, legs spreading to hold them up. The casual strength stole his breath, his sense. The way they fit together made him shake, made him hump hard. This was maddening, the way they moved together and things just faded away. Ice made him forget his responsibilities, his worries. Ice made him want.

It was dangerous.

Dangerous and amazing.

The noise that exploded in his head just then couldn't be ignored. Twenty or more dragons set up a cry, the sound better than a klaxon alarm.

"Ice!" He landed on the floor, took off at a run. "Damien! Damien, fly! Fly!"

Damien's roar answered him, and Ice followed him, footsteps pounding after him. "Keon. Pants."

"Fuck that. Those are our babies!"

Ice grunted, but when he looked back, Ice was right there, pants on. Nice. The man was a professional.

He came skittering to a halt, Sergei Volon right there in the cavern and trying to carry little Krystal and Chi out the front door.

"Don't you dare. I will fry your ass where you stand," Keon shouted, feeling Damien's fire building up in his chest and belly.

"You will not hurt your dragons," Sergei sneered.

"Chi!" Ice roared his dragon's name, barreling past him, right at the asshole trying to steal the babies.

Ice! Chi reached for his bonded, waves of cold pouring off him.

"Better dead than a commodity." He threw a thought back to the adolescents. *The hatchling. We must protect the hatchling.*

The dragons answered with varying degrees of coherence, but it was Ice who slammed into the Russian like a runner sliding into third, Chi landing on Ice's shoulder. When Krystal went reeling through the air, Keon leaped for her.

I got you, baby, he thought, then heard the click of a hammer, the weapon pointed at Ice's head.

"You're bringing in mercenaries now?" Sergei sneered. "That is not acceptable. We're going to take over, Keon. There's no need for guardians anymore. You'll give me the beasts, or I'll kill him."

"Fuck that shit, Keon. He's not gonna kill me." Ice simply stared Sergei down, not appearing worried at all.

"Of course he's not." Keon gathered the hatchling to him

and called out for Damien, for that heat and fire and strength. Damien answered, more power slamming through him, pouring from his eyes and mouth, the flame of the dragon his to use, to control.

One scream sounded before Sergei disappeared, melted to a grease spot.

Then the whole world went black, Damien's roar inside him.

He spent his last moment awake hoping that Ice really was his other half and had managed to survive the attack.

Holy shit. Holy fucking shit. Ice stared at the spot that had been a man for about ten solid seconds. Then he lifted his arm, checking in with Chi, who'd slid down to his wrist.

Ice. Iceiceice. Bad man. Bad man came.

All the others were staring at him, wings fluttering, obviously scared. "I know, baby. He's gone." He went to Keon, kneeling by the lean, naked body. Keon was breathing, skin feverish, so Ice pulled him close, cooling Keon off. He kissed the sluggish pulse beating at the base of Keon's throat. "Wake up, baby."

The little ones needed reassurance, and he needed to know what had just happened. They moved closer, crying out, moaning, calling for Keon.

"Damien? Help me?" Ice called out, hoping it would work.

It was little Chi who came though, little blue body draped over Keon's forehead, dropping the fever, and those dark eyes opened. "The babies?"

"They're all right. They need you, though. They're scared." He helped Keon sit up.

"No. No, you're okay. We're here. We have you." Keon's arms opened up, and the little ones came flocking.

"Who was that guy?" Ice had seen him dropping something off the other night, had seen the argument he and Keon had.

"Sergei. He brings me eggs they find in the old Soviet Union.

He's found so many lately."

"Who is this 'we' he mentioned. Shutting you down?" This was a whole new development, someone else knowing about the dragons besides Ice and his backers.

"I have no idea. Why would anyone want to do that?"

God, sometimes he forgot how naive Keon was, how isolated.

"Well, 'we' is a bad thing in wet work, babe. It's like cockroaches. Shutting you down would require a lot of folks."

"I've been here one hundred and fifty years and no one has hurt us. What is wet work? We're not wet. I mean, the pool is wet..."

"Black ops, baby. Or the black market." Ice chewed his lip. He could see why people thought these dragons could be weapons. Keon had vaporized the Russian dude before Ice could tell him no bullet could penetrate the ice barrier he could create given the warning he'd had. Hell, Keon was the fucking dangerous one. "We're gonna need backup if we want to get to the bottom of this."

"No. No strangers. We have to protect the children."

"My team aren't strangers." No, they were family, and he was going to leave them behind forever soon, so he would call them in.

The huge form of Damien landed in front of the big front door, the one Sergei had broken down. *There are others. Watching. Waiting.*

Ice frowned mightily. One, he shouldn't be able to hear Damien's actual thoughts, and two, fuck! This was gonna get hairy. "How close?"

Two days. Three. They wait for the return of the bad one. Images of Jeeps, of a handful of soldiers, weapons flashed in his mind.

"Crap." He would call in his team ASAP.

"We'll close everything down, keep the babies in."

"I'll get a message to Gig. My guys can be here in less than a day."

"I… We've never had to bring in an army."

"How old are you again?" Ice stared, stunned at how Keon could be so self-contained.

"One hundred and fifty-seven. How old are you?"

"Thirty-two." One hundred and -- Jesus. He sat down, making Chi squawk when they hit the hard stone floor.

"Are you okay? Ice?" Keon -- still naked as a jaybird -- wrapped around him. "Damien? Is he sick?"

He has trouble believing your age.

"Am I supposed to be able to hear your dragon?"

"I hear all the dragons. Guardians hear all the dragons."

"I heard them all yelling."

"You must be a Guardian."

"What does that mean?" Ice hugged Keon tight. "Ah, fuck it, I was planning to stay anyway."

"Oh, good. Chi insisted you would. He's very determined." Keon rested hard against him.

"Uh-huh. Well, he ought to know, right? Bonded as we are."

"Yes." Keon's eyes were red, bloodshot. "I'm tired, Ice. It's hard, holding Damien inside me."

"I'll help, okay?" Ice kissed Keon's temple. "I'll put a call in to my team, and I can keep watch while you sleep until we get help in."

"You swear they won't hurt them, the babies?"

"I'll kill them myself first." He guessed there was something to this whole guardian thing. That fire in his belly was all protective rage. And a healthy dose of lust. Now that the battle was over, he needed Keon like he needed air.

The baby dragons skittered off, calling to Damien, and Ice took a kiss from Keon, mashing those soft lips with his. He wanted Keon, wanted to spread the man out and fuck him. Right there on the floor.

"Hard."

"Hell, yes." Ice was hard as stone, his cock aching.

"No, babe. The floor is hard."

"Oh." He chuckled, rolling to put Keon on top of him. "Better?"

Keon blinked down at him, then grinned. "As long as you're okay."

"I just need to come, baby." He arched up, letting Keon feel the hard length of his cock. "Open my pants."

Thankfully, Keon had faced down their enemy naked, so it was just a matter of unzipping Ice's fatigues and getting them rubbing together. They kissed over and over, until Ice felt like he might explode, the heat spreading through him, warming his always-cold body.

"I can work with this." Keon said it against his mouth, then sat up, grabbing both their cocks, rubbing them madly.

Arching, Ice pushed hard, needing that friction. The stone under his back warmed, the volcano under them almost as hot as the dragon-fed heat of Keon above him. Ice grunted, humping hard, his spine tingling with his impending orgasm.

"Wait for me," Keon moaned, falling forward to kiss him again, tongue pushing into Ice's mouth. A little aggression from Keon went a long way toward making him want to scream.

Ice grabbed Keon's ass, yanking them together so hard their skin made an erotic slapping noise.

Keon's head came up, those pretty, dark eyes wide, and Keon came for him, wet heat spreading on his belly. Ice grunted, his orgasm bursting through him, his breath caught in his throat. Oh, fuck. Fuck yes. All that battle tension drained right out of him, leaving him limp and sated.

"Oh, baby. Better, huh? Think maybe I should stay for a while?"

Keon's fingers twined with his, and then his lover was asleep, boneless in his arms.

Ice guessed that was a yes.

He grinned, thinking this suicide mission may not have ended his life, but it had sure changed the direction. He stood, pulling Keon up and carrying him to the bedroom where he'd left his gear.

Time to make that call to his guys. He needed them for one last op.

Teamwork

Chapter One

Keon's head pounded furiously, his brain banging against his skull, protesting the way that he'd channeled dragon fire and let it blast through him. He needed to nap a little longer. At least he thought he'd napped. Maybe passed out.

"Did you call your team?" he asked Ice, who sat next to him on the floor.

"Uh-huh. They're coming. You look like shit, baby." Those icy blue eyes moved over him, Ice obviously worried.

"I'm a little drained." He patted Ice's leg, listening to Damien rumble. His dragon was furious -- both because of the small army of soldiers waiting in the town at the base of the mountains for Sergei to return, which you know, tough to do after being reduced to a grease spot, and because someone had been in the keep, had tried to hurt the babies.

No one hurt his clutch. No one.

Ice tugged him up and stood, lifting him. "Come on, baby. Jeez, I don't even know where you sleep, really."

"No? What kind of boyfriend are you?" He had to tease. They were more like... dragon-bonded fuckbuddies. Right?

"Uh, well, up 'til now I've always been a sucky one. We'll see how it works with you." Ice's pale eyebrows gyrated.

He pointed to the huge doorway that marked his rooms. The bed was huge and soft, the fireplace always blazing.

"Wow. Way nicer than Chi's little sleeping area." Ice put him down on the bed.

"I live here. You were an uninvited guest. Now we'll make sure you're comfortable, too."

"Gonna keep me?" Ice stripped off, reminding Keon that he'd faced the bad guy naked. That had to be macho on his part, right?

"Uh-huh."

"Good deal." Ice grimaced. "My team might be pissed. We just lost one team member a few weeks ago. Now me, as well?"

"How many are coming and are they going to shoot me? I don't like that." It had happened a few times in his tenure as dragon guardian and it wasn't fun.

"No shooting allowed. There should be five. No, four. Spider is the one who left. Jacques, who we call One-Eyed Jack. He's a Cajun. Gig is the tech guy. Shannon is the big Irishman, and there's our surveillance guy, Chino."

"Is Ice your real name?" Had he slept with a man whose name he didn't know? No. No, they hadn't slept at all. They'd fucked.

"No." Ice shrugged. "We all have call signs. Mine is as much my name now as any, I guess."

That explained why little Chi had used that when he and Ice had bonded then. Whatever name Ice used for himself was the name baby dragon Chi would understand.

"My name is really just Keon, just like my father and my grandfather."

"No shit? I'm not named after anyone. I was three months old when someone dropped me off at a local Catholic church." Ice sounded so matter-of-fact.

"I was taken to learn how to take care of the babies at five, but life was different then." The middle of the nineteenth century had seen many children pressed into labor and he'd been lucky, blessed.

"I guess so. How have you lived so long, man? Not to be nosy, but, well, I am nosy."

"It's the dragons. They can't live without their bonded, so we live as long as they do. You'll live until Chi dies and he has hundreds of years left to him."

"Wow." Ice seemed to mull that over, chewing his lower lip. "What about Damien?"

"He's in his prime. We have at least six hundred good years before we start to get tired." And then they'd settle in, spend a near eternity quiet and lazy. Maybe he'd get fat.

"Holy shit." Ice blinked, vibrating a little, his skin going two shades paler. "That's... Seriously?"

"As far as I know, yes. I mean, accidents happen, but when the couple I replaced went to ground, they'd been active for nearly a millennium." Was that bad?

Ice grunted like he'd been hit. Huh. Maybe it was a lot to take in.

"It's good, right? To be long-lived and healthy? You don't even have to steal people's souls or suck blood." He had books. He knew about vampires and stuff.

"No, it's good. That many years are just hard to imagine." Ice grinned. "Uh, can two full-size dragons live together?"

"They can. They aren't territorial, surprisingly. They like family units." It was just hard, to find places like this, to find humans to bind to, to fly without being caught and killed.

"Oh, cool. I mean, who knows, you could kick me and Chi out tomorrow."

"Why?" He'd never met another bonded person, not in years. This might be the best thing to happen in his lifetime.

"I don't know? I drop my towels on the floor. Sometimes I hum movie themes in my sleep."

"Oh. I saw a movie once." There had been singing and

dancing and a man made from straw.

"Once?" Ice appeared horrified. "Baby. We have to get you a TV."

"Okay. We've done well here, really. I have electricity. Normal appliances. Running water."

"Baby, your stove is from 1962." Ice was laughing at him, those icy blue-gray eyes dancing. Ice looked happy. That was a damned good thing.

They settled together in the blankets, Keon's eyelids so heavy, so tired. It was warm here, comfortable, familiar.

Rest, beloved. There will be more men coming. His dragon's mental voice was fuzzy with sleep.

"More men coming." He murmured the words, Damien's call as strong as Ice's, drawing him down and down.

"I know. Don't worry, baby. We got this." Ice stroked his cheeks, patting a little.

"Got this. My Ice."

And with that he was sound asleep, body's energy used up.

"Ice just called us in." Gig looked completely shocked, like he couldn't believe what he'd heard.

Jacques, on the other hand, whooped a little. "Oooeee. I knew he wouldn't just leave us behind."

"Uh-huh," Gig said. "I'll let you explain to him why it took us twenty minutes to get to him, not the twenty-four hours he expects."

"Nah, we can sit for a bit." They had eyes on the strike force that was camped out, anyway. Might as well gather all the intel they could. Jacques liked to be prepared.

There was some big thing going on up here on the mountain, some bad juju, and they needed to know everything they could going in. That way Ice was way less likely to kick their asses.

Gig chuckled. "He's still the team leader, huh?"

"Yeah." Though things still seemed... weird. Everything was in fucking flux and Jacques didn't approve. Acting team leader he might be, but he wasn't all that good at giving orders. "Everyone go on and get camp broke. We headin' to see the man in a few hours."

They'd go fix whatever needing fixin' and then he was bringing their leader home, damn it.

Ice had given them the call. Surely that meant the man was ready to go. Right?

Chapter Two

Ice watched Keon sleep, pondering six hundred years. Holy shit, that was a long time. Like, a long-long time. Keon was so matter-of-fact about it, too. No worries, no stress. I've seen a movie.

Christ.

Was that gonna be him in a century? Completely out of touch? Not that he was in the flow too much now. He grinned. He only watched movies because Gig got bored and put them on streaming. Still, he could show Keon so much. They could spend years learning each other.

Ice? Ice? Keon? Pool? Yes? One of the bigger females stuck her head around the arched doorway. *Pool? Yes?*

Keon nodded, moaned and curled close. "Just watch the babies."

Ice was going to have to get them a door. A curtain. Something.

"Come on, Gala. We'll go to the pool. Can Chi come?" Ice rolled out of bed.

Swimming! We go swim with Ice! Chi's little voice was like a bell.

He chuckled. "Come on. Only two more little ones." If he didn't put limits on it, everyone would crowd to the bathing room.

One of the older ones brought the tiny-tiny newborn, carefully putting her in bed with Keon, who immediately drew her close. Ice shook his head. Keon was damned good at what he did.

"Krystal want to come?" She'd been one of the ones Sergei

tried to take. She probably needed some reassurance.

Now that he could hear all of them, buzzing and chattering, it was like being dropped in the center of a daycare -- laughter and playing and talking. They all clomped down to the pool, the shuffle-drag sound so familiar already.

Chi was on his shoulder, tail around his neck. *My Ice. My bonded. Mine. Mine. So good. So mine. IceIceIce.*

Yep. Monkey.

Chi nipped his ear. *Dragon.*

"Lizard." He said it out loud, sliding into the shallow end of the big pool. Oh. God, that felt good.

The others played happily, the older dragons surprisingly attentive, careful of the little ones. They really were a family. Ice was impressed. He liked being part of a team; it suited him. From Elemental Ops to dragon guardian.

Chi did somersaults in the water, calling out. *Look, Ice. Watch!*

Good boy! Ice watched, listening with half an ear for any calls, any warnings. His guys would take a few hours, and Ice needed to remain alert.

Eventually they tired out, piling together in front of the fire at the back of the chamber, grooming each other. Chi went from one dragon to Ice, back to another dragon.

It's okay, Chi. Love on your denmates. He wasn't jealous, and Chi needed to know it was okay to be what he was.

Chi's pointed face slid against his. *Beloved.*

Then he was off again, bounce bounce bounce.

Ice chuckled, leaning back and floating a little, letting the hot water seep into his bones.

Okay, this may be the most wonderful invention in history. Better than a hot tub, this had to be a volcanic hot springs. He wondered if he could get Keon out here in the deep of the night. Alone. Riding him.

He thumped himself. Be good.

Virtuous.

He was on watch. With the dragons.

Ice. Ice. Strangers. Strangers coming. Damien's voice was a deep, vicious growl, the image of his team sharp and clear in his mind.

Safe. Damien, safe. The last thing he needed was Damien frying his guys. "Damn, I have to put on clothes." He got out of the pool, thankful that Keon had left towels.

Ice. They're coming. Keon sleeps so deep.

I will make sure everyone is safe. These are my friends. You watch over Keon, he told Damien. It took a huge effort to haul his ass out of the pool, but he did it, and Chi brought him clothes, the brilliant beast. "Such a good boy."

Good dragon. I come meet people?

Yes. Come with me. He pulled on the pants and T-shirt, and then held out his arm for Chi. Might as well start out like he was gonna hold out.

Chi hopped right up, settling with a happy little trill. He thought of the meeting. Guys, amazing brilliant dragon boy that sings to me and needs me. Chi, guys.

Lord.

He headed to the main entrance to the cavern, the one that looked like the door to a mine shack. It was amazing how normal the place appeared at first glance. All the dragons were gone, disappeared, hiding away and silent. Chi chittered softly, the sound worried.

"I promise, kiddo, no one will hurt you. You'll love Gig."

Gig. Chi tried the name out in his little voice.

He opened the door, slowly, eyes on the guys, on the possible danger. He knew they would have signaled him if they were under duress, but these days, with the stress they were under, anyone could have a hair trigger.

"'Bout time you called us in," Jacques drawled, his one good eye gleaming in the fading light.

"Ice has always been a drama llama." Gig stared at him. "Is that an iguana?"

Ice chuckled when Chi flapped and hissed. "No. You guys have to promise me you'll be good or you can't come in."

"Good?" Shannon tilted his head, blinked. "Are we ever good?"

"You guys are always damned good, but this is a delicate situation." He stroked Chi's chin. "This, guys, is a dragon."

All the guys just stopped, stared. Jacques appeared appalled, his mouth screwing up with disbelief.

Chi preened, his little blue self all puffed up. He deflated a bit when Ice said, "He's just a baby."

"He's on your shoulders. Is that safe?" Gig was a worrywart.

"Oh, yeah. I mean, he bites, but luckily he likes me."

Chi chittered at him, making the guys all blink.

"So, uh, come in. No sense tempting fate with a strike team out there."

"Hey, now, is there room for us in the... uh... cave?" One-Eyed Jack looked worried as hell, trying to size everything up like he always did, coming up with numbers that didn't match.

"Fuck, yes. Come on, you idiots." Ice headed back inside, knowing he had to be normal. The guys were already freaked out, and it would just get worse.

The little ones were cute, but Damien was... mind-blowing.

Hell, Serena had almost shorted him out, and she was half Damien's size.

"Whoa. It's like a TARDIS in *Dr. Who*." Gig stared at the way the cavern opened up.

"It's a good place. Needs some reinforcements, though."

Shannon snapped to attention at the prospect of something to do, something the team understood. "What are you thinking, boss?"

"The Russian walked right in the front door, with a gun, like it was nothing."

"Russian?" Jack was checking out the main room, peering down each cut out hall. When he got to what Ice had discovered was Damien's hall, a deep warning growl sounded.

Jack jumped back, weapon coming to bear, and Ice walked over, sticking his head into the corridor. "Sorry, Damien. Just us.

You'll let me know when you're ready to meet everyone?"

Damien answered with what felt like a touch to his brain, a fond caress.

Ice grinned. "Don't go down there, Jack."

"What the fuck is going on?" His team gathered together, staring at him as one man, letting Jack talk for them.

"Come on, let's go to the kitchen, at least. I need coffee." He led the way, listening to their boots hit the rock behind him. He was barefoot, damp, wearing soft gauzy pants and a T-shirt of Keon's. Yay. They had to think he'd lost his mind. Maybe he had, but he knew where he was going to stay. Right here with his mate and the dragons.

"What the fuck is this place, man?" Shannon sounded worried. "Are there animals here?"

Chi made more scolding noises, and Ice grimaced. "Dragons, Shan. I told you. I know it doesn't make sense, but then, neither did Spider's were-buddies."

"Drag-ons?" Gig asked. "As in, more than the wee one on your shoulders, *Lord of the Rings*, oh my God you have a lair of dragons?"

"Uh. Yeah." He put water in the coffee maker, got grounds measured out. "Welcome to the possible biological weapon I was sent to dismantle."

Weapon? Chi whispered. *What's weapon?*

Not you, baby boy.

Ice. Those tiny wings fluttered for him, the sound comforting deep in his soul.

"Weapon, *cher?* What can they do? Scratch me to death?" Jack was staring at Chi, his one good eye glittering fiercely, the gold taking over the green.

"That's probably not their first instinct, no." Keon appeared, pale as a ghost, hair like something out of a Japanese horror flick.

"Shit!" Chino jumped about a mile "Where did you come from, man?"

"I was sleeping. Where did you come from?"

"These are my team, Keon." Ice went to his new lover, drawn to him, wanting to support him if he fell, which he looked like he would.

"Your team. Welcome. Would you like coffee?"

Ice smiled. So polite, his Keon, so precise.

"We'd love some," Jack said, pouring on the Cajun charm. "Dis'a helluva place you got here."

"It is. It's a good home." Keon looked at the crew. "I only have three cups."

"We all came with our ready gear," Shannon said. "We have cups. Gig?"

Gig glanced at all of them, then rolled his eyes. "Aw, man, why do I always get shit duty? Be right back."

"I think that there are cookies." Keon bustled around, and Ice watched him, making sure he didn't keel over.

"I like cookies," Gig said, coming in with cups. "Do dragons eat cookies?"

"Dragons do eat cookies. Chi loves cheese. He's a cheese thief."

Ice grinned because Chi chanted in his head. *Cheesecheesecheese.*

"You'll have to ask Keon. He controls the cheese," he told Chi. Chi fluttered over, head-butting Keon.

Keon chuckled. "Mooch." The little dragon was cuddled close, held and rocked, and fed a bite of cheese, and Ice had to grin. Had to. Keon was such a mom.

Everyone was staring at him, looking gobsmacked.

"We should feed you, huh?" Ice didn't know what else to do.

"Cookies. Coffee. Right." Keon got moving again, dragging out supplies.

"We have, uh, apple pie MREs," Shannon said.

Keon wrinkled his nose. "I have supplies. They bring them from town."

"They who?" Jack's one-eyed gaze sharpened even more, now that he had something to focus on. "Who else has access?"

"Friends of my family, people that own the market." Keon shrugged. "They come every few weeks with the groceries."

"Would they talk? Tell anyone what you got going on?"

"I doubt it. We've been here for years. Decades. Centuries." Keon was beginning to panic, his eyes wild, and Ice put a hand on Keon's back.

"Enough," Ice finally said. "You guys stink. Eat and I'll show you where you can bathe."

"I… Put them in the…" Keon looked at him, pale as milk. "I don't know."

"Hey." He caught Keon around the waist. "Back to bed, you. Eat up, guys. Watch the cheese." Keon had expended too much energy. He needed to go back to sleep.

"I don't want to be rude, but --" Keon's dark eyes rolled up in his head and Ice's lover collapsed.

"Shit!" Jacques sprinted over, their Jack of all trades also their team medic. "Let me look at him."

"He's tired."

"He's exhausted. The man's carryin' bags enough for a three-day cruise." Jack glared at Ice. "What you been doin' to him?"

Ice scowled back. "The nasty, among other things."

"Lalala, not listening." Gig covered his ears, which made Chi chitter with laughter. Silly beast.

Ice hefted Keon and headed back to the bedroom, Jacques behind them, and Chi too, flapping and galumphing.

"Damien? Is he all right?" He knew the bond with the big dragon allowed Damien to know things.

Tired. Worried. Mostly so tired.

I'll take care of him, Big Guy. I promise.

I know. He could hear the trust in Damien's thought.

"Who are you talking to, boss?"

"The big dragon. You'll meet him. Keon wore himself out fighting the Russian. Can you just check all his vitals, Jack?"

"The big dragon." Jack stared at him, lips pursed. "Seriously?"

"You'll see. I didn't have time to be a skeptic. I bonded with

Chi my first day here."

My Ice. Chi climbed up Jack's body, chittering. *My Ice. Mine. My best Ice.*

"Uh. *Cher?* Is he supposed to do this?" Jacques held stock still, staring at Chi's little blue form.

"Yep." Ice cackled. "You need to get used to them."

"Is he a baby?"

"He is. Wee. The hatchling is tiny. I'll show you."

Jack nodded, but moved to check Keon's vitals. Ice couldn't wait to see what Jack said about the man's body temp. Good thing his men were all Elemental Ops.

"He's burning up. Burning up, man. 108. 109, now."

"Shit." That was a lot. Ice came in at the low nineties, and Spider had never spiked at more than 105. "Damien?"

Touch him. Balance him.

Oh. Right!

Ice gave Jack a little shove. "Hold my dragon, huh?" He slid into the bed with Keon, wrapping around him.

"Ice." Keon sighed his name, so hot in his arms.

"Damien told me what to do, baby."

"Okay." No worry, no stress, just a nod and a smile and Keon relaxed into him. Keon's heat seeped into him, warming his cold hands and feet.

Jack took Keon's temp again, right in the ear. "104. Rock on, Iceman."

"Yeah. I'm good at icy."

Keon inhaled deeply, chest rising and falling. Relaxing. Thank God. Poor guy had taken on some heat.

"This whole thing is deep fucked, *cher.* There's a little dragon guy and you got a Japanese dude wrapped around you."

"Japanese?" He pulled back just enough to peer at Keon. "Anime, maybe."

"Somebody not Cajun, for sure."

He chuckled. "For sure. Hey, can you get the guys to set up a perimeter? Chi, can you get Serena to show them the bathing room? I bet she'll like Gig a lot."

"You've got a girl here?"

Chi made the most amazing sound, almost like a human giggle. *Serena! Serena come show them big dragon!*

Chi? Keon? Ice? Is it safe?

It was still so, so weird to hear their little voices in his head.

He heard Keon in his head, too. *It's fine. They're with Ice.*

Serena and Tatiana came in, the older girls too big to fit through the door together, triangular heads bobbing, eyes bright. Serena had rich red-orange scales, while Tatiana was nearly purple.

"Oh, dear God." Jack was going to collapse, swaying, all color draining from his face.

"Hey, ladies." Ice grinned, looking at the beautiful girls. "Are you hungry?"

Serena's head tilted. *Playing. Show the men to the water?*

Yes, please, love. Ice already felt so close to all of the dragons.

She came to him, cheek sliding against his, so gentle, then she turned, yawned, showing all her teeth while Tatiana headbutted Jack, hard.

"They're showing off for you, buddy. Kinda makes your balls try to crawl up in your body, huh?"

"Lawd, yes. They mean?" Jack was rubbing his head, his good eye squinty as hell.

"Not if you're nice to them. Jacques is my friend, Serena. Be easy."

She hissed softly, tail swishing as she nudged Jack, got him moving as Tatiana headed to round up the others.

"Be good, Jack," Ice called, letting more of Keon's heat escape into him.

He could feel Serena's soft, happy laughter. She was so full of energy, so vibrant. Their sweet family.

Whoa.

When had that happened?

Ice chuckled when Keon patted his back, soothing him

without even knowing why. He had a family. A lizard family.

Not a lizard. Chi could sound so offended. Grr and argh and cute as hell.

My gorgeous dragon.

The wave of pride and joy made him a little dizzy. He hugged Keon close and let his eyes drift shut. His guys were on duty, even if they didn't understand what was going on. He could rest.

Keon sighed softly, one hand around his hip, holding on.

Yeah. Rest.

Chapter Three

Jacques thought he might just die, his head hurt so bad. He'd followed Ice down a rabbit hole to Neverland or somethin'. That had to be the only explanation. Dragons? Caves that went deep into the mountain? Jesu Cristo.

Something whispered in his mind, too. Something that had a feminine voice, something begging him to notice. He ignored it, because that was what a man did when he started hearing voices. He fucking ignored them.

The two big dragon bodies swayed in front of him, and Jack followed, putting one foot in front of the other with dogged determination. His fucking head was gonna explode. Boom. Splat. Then what would the team do? They done lost Spider, and he had a feeling Ice would be staying here in this crazy as hell place.

The dragons lead him to a huge cavern, one he couldn't have imagined when he stood outside. The place had three or four pools of lots of sizes, and steam rose from all of them. Steam. Now, that he could understand. His element, steam. His own personal talent.

Jacques ignored all the dragons, their scaly bodies and bright colors like something out of a movie. He'd been in the field for weeks. Time to wash off the grime.

One thing at a time. The situation would have to be dealt with, but not now.

Maybe the steam would help his fucking head.

Keon moaned and stretched, his body sliding against Ice's.

Oh. Better.

Much better.

He'd been so tired he'd been hallucinating, lost. Now he felt like he was fitting in his own skin again. Ice had sucked the heat right out of him, the fever that had taken hold of his body. No one had ever been there for him like Ice had.

Keon cracked an eye, admiring the length of long, hard body, the way Ice looked against his sheets. In his bed. He reached out with one finger, tracing the muscled ridges in the flat belly. Ice had such pale skin, the abs so defined, so perfect.

Ice hummed, turning toward him.

He couldn't stop touching, even if it woke Ice up.

"Mmm. Hey." Ice's pale blue eyes popped open, the expression in them fond.

"Hey." Oh, so pretty. So fine. His.

"You feeling better?"

"So much. I feel good. There are lots of people here, hmm?" Too many to risk touching, he guessed.

"They're bathing." Ice nuzzled his chin.

"Bathing." He lifted his head, offering Ice his throat.

"Yep." Ice nipped at him, the sting almost cold.

The tiny pain crawled along his skin. "More, please."

"Oh, you sure you're up to it, baby? Damien was worried."

He took Ice's hand, brought it to his cock, which was enjoying how close Ice was.

"You're definitely up." Ice stroked him, up and down.

"Feel better. Please, love. More." He wanted to fly, to feel Ice all around him, making him come.

"I can do that." Ice kissed him, tongue pushing into his mouth. One kiss melted into another and then another. They stole his breath, made his heart pound and he pushed closer. He rolled Ice to his back, climbing aboard those lean hips.

Ice laughed, hands sliding up his thighs. "Hungry man. I like it."

"Good. I want you." He flattened his hands on Ice's chest, those tight nipples digging into his palms, all hard points.

"Come and get me." Ice was all grins and come-hither looks, tongue flicking out to wet his lips.

"Uh-huh." Keon kissed that sexy mouth, ready and willing to eat Ice up. Ice wrapped one hand around the back of his head, fingers digging in, holding them together. The man knew how to kiss, so good, so deep, making Keon's lips burn.

Burning, Ice. The thought made him chuckle, which got him a hard little pinch, one that stung all the way down.

"No laughing in bed, baby. I might get a complex."

"Just thinking that you made me burn. Crazy, huh?" He reached down, petting Ice's belly, teasing the very tip of Ice's cock.

"It is. This whole thing is nuts." Ice touched him back, fingers playing on his ribs, over his hip, making his skin tingle. "I like it."

"Oh, good." He wasn't sure what he would do if Ice didn't.

"Uh-huh." Ice rolled up to bite his nipple. "Reward me for being a good Guardian and sticking around, huh?"

"I can do that." He kept moving his hand south, fully intending to wrap his fingers around the man's cock.

"Oh, baby. I want that hot mouth of yours. Get me good and wet." Ice pushed him down gently, hands on his shoulders.

He hummed as he went, licking and sucking at each piece of skin that passed his lips. Finally, blessedly, Ice's dick was right there, pushing at his mouth. He opened up and took it in, tongue sliding along the underside so he could taste. The flavor was at once brand-new and perfectly familiar, so he moaned and opened up for more.

Ice felt cold, but not unpleasantly so. In fact, it was a little like sucking a Popsicle. Keon moaned and wrapped his lips around the base, pulling hard all the way up.

Humming, Ice pushed both hands into Keon's hair, tugging a little at his scalp, making goose bumps rise. "Oh, that's good, baby. Real good."

He nodded, repeated the gesture again and again, sucking slow and hard. This was something he could really get into, a pleasurable task, for sure. Ice made amazing noises, sex sounds that were rough and sharp and hungry.

Keon let his eyes drop closed, focusing on the drag of Ice's cock on his tongue. The feel of it was like nothing else, and he liked the powerful sensation of holding this man captive by his prick. Ice's fingers tangled in his hair, holding on, rubbing his scalp. The massage made him moan and relax his jaw so he could take more. He went all the way down to the root, the tip sliding into his throat.

"Oh, fuck. Baby. So good." Ice petted him, praised him, out loud and in his head like a dragon.

In his head.

The touch was so different than theirs. Ice's voice was like a balm. Like the cool taste of mint on a hot day. Something only his.

He buried his nose in Ice's soft curls, swallowing over and over.

"Keon. Want to fuck you, baby. Want you to ride me. Need your heat."

He let Ice's cock go reluctantly, the flavor an addiction.

"Come on and ride me." Ice pulled him up for a kiss, feeding his oral needs.

It was easy to rock down, rub Ice's wet tip against his hole, slicking himself up. He was still pretty stretched, reminding him that this was all happening so fast. He hadn't known Ice, only days ago and now?

Ice was inside him.

Pushing deep, Ice slipped right in, wet and perfect, like a key to his lock.

He moaned, rocking, ass sliding on Ice's thighs.

"So pretty." Ice stroked his belly and hips, then his cock.

"Want to feel you, everywhere." He hadn't wanted anyone so much. Ever.

"Anything, baby. Anything you want." Ice pressed his cock, thumb pushing against the slit, and his eyes crossed, electricity jolting through him.

He rocked, his hips pulling up then pushing down. The burn in his ass made him pant. His muscles were buzzing, working as he drove himself onto Ice's cock.

"More." Ice stroked his dick, up and down.

"More," he agreed, bracing himself on Ice's chest. When Ice's other hand landed on his hip, yanking good and hard, the friction got amazing.

All he could do was grit his teeth and bounce, riding hard, that heavy cock piercing him. He clamped down with his muscles, urging Ice on, faster and harder.

"Baby." Ice rolled up, hips slamming into him, driving deep.

"Close," Keon said, his breath coming fast and hard. Close was maybe an underestimate, because he shot. Boom. He glanced down, watching his seed spreading on Ice's skin.

"Hot." Ice moaned, slamming into him two, three more times before the man filled him deep inside, the tingles surprising him all over. Magic. This was magic and he wanted to feel it, again and again.

"Keeping you," he said. He patted Ice's chest, feeling clumsy.

"Good. Where else am I gonna raise Chi?"

"Nowhere. This is a safe place." He stopped, frowned. "It is still safe for the babies, isn't it?"

"We'll make sure it is." Ice looked serious. "This is the best environment for them."

"They're why this place exists. It's our calling." The dragons were inside them.

"I guess it is at that. Is that why you and I are already family?"

"I suppose? I've never heard another person inside me. Have you?"

"No, baby." Ice laughed. "I even knew a guy who was a telepath and he said my head was like a block of ice."

"No. No, you're inside me, like a song."

"I hear you, too." Ice leaned up, kissing him.

The connection was electric, making him buzz. He lapped at Ice's lips, energy flowing through him. Oh, delicious. He moaned and squeezed Ice, the sweet prick trapped inside him.

"Gonna get me going again, baby." Ice gripped his hips, eyes so blue and bright with desire.

"That's not a bad thing."

"Nope. Just warning you." Ice rolled him to his back, smiling down at him.

He gasped, the casual strength making him ache. He loved how damned fine Ice was, how beautiful, muscles flexing under his skin. He loved this man already and he didn't even know if Ice liked pizza.

At least he knew the man liked cheese and his ass. Consecutively, not concurrently.

He laughed out loud, and Ice thrust up inside him, hard enough to make him grunt. "What did I say about laughing, Keon?"

"Bad for… for your ego. Do that again."

"Over and over, I promise." Ice gave it to him, really making friction.

Keon gritted his teeth and fought the urge to cry out. He was super-sensitive now, his whole body on fire. Ice was like the best kind of frozen dessert.

His own personal Popsicle.

A bomb pop. He'd had those once when Jenny brought them up from the store.

He was going to laugh again.

"You're an evil man, baby." Ice was laughing now, too. Maybe he'd seen what was in Keon's head.

"Evil? Dragons only bond with good humans." He hoped. Ice had to be a good man.

"Uh-huh. You're a bad man."

"Me?" Ice's cock pegged something deep inside him, lighting a flame.

"Yep. So bad you're burning me up. I love it."

They were ridiculous. Ridiculous and that silly fire felt so real. He loved the way Ice's body moved, the way those eyes watched him so carefully.

He moaned, rocked up against that sweet fucking cock.

Ice pushed and pushed, really giving it to him. The man fucked like a machine, making Keon whimper and clutch at those wide shoulders.

Low cries tore from him, his entire body focused on nothing but this. He wrapped his legs around Ice's hips, surprised at how weak they were from kneeling over Ice's hips like he had.

"I got you, baby." The words twined around his heart, holding him, helping him.

"I know." He reached up, touching Ice's cheek, and Ice turned his head, lips brushing his palm.

He didn't expect the little flashes of romance from a hard warrior like Ice. His body tightened, squeezed, clenching on Ice's cock.

"Fuck. Oh, fuck baby."

Oh, that was good so he did it again. And then again. Ice pounded him, muscles flexing, jaw clenched. His abs tightened and he could barely breathe. He was gonna lose it again, his balls up and tight, his dick smooshed between him and Ice.

"Ice." He grabbed Ice's ass, tugged hard.

"Gonna, baby. Can't wait this time."

"Uh-huh." Keon was addicted to the sensation, the flash of cold inside him.

Ice was sweating. Sweating. He did that, made his frozen lover come alive. Ice grinned at him, baring his teeth like a dragon, and came for him again, deep inside him.

That little sting of cold was all he needed to come himself. He shouted, his body arching under Ice, his balls aching from his second orgasm. The tiny pain maddened him, made him thrash, the pleasure too intense.

Ice's eyes watched every second, the fierce pleasure one more dimension.

Keon cradled Ice when they slumped together, stroking the long, lean line of Ice's back.

Ice kissed his throat, then his mouth. "I don't know about you, but I feel better."

"Tons." He couldn't stop smiling.

"Good. You had me worried."

"It's hard, to let Damien in like that."

Ice propped up on one elbow. "How does it happen?"

He thought about that a second. "You open up, and that will pours through you. It's vast."

"I bet." Ice chuckled. "Chi is small yet."

"The first time is scary, then it's just… exhausting." He chewed on his bottom lip. "It burns."

"Well, that's why you have me." Ice pondered a moment, head tilting. "You think Chi will shoot ice?"

"I do. He's special. My only blue baby."

"He's glorious." Ice got this goofy expression on his face.

"He is. He's so funny, so quick."

"Is Damien funny?" The chance to pillow talk with Ice was priceless. His lover was so relaxed.

"He's wicked. He makes me laugh with his meanness."

"I found him very calming when you were out of it." Ice sighed. "I ought to make sure Serena isn't picking her teeth with Jack. He seemed to make her a little grumpy."

"No one's fussing, I'd hear."

"Would I?" Ice kissed his cheek. "What happens now?"

"Do I need to send Damien to burn them?" He didn't want to, but he would, for the babies.

"No. I think there's another way." Ice seemed so sure of his team.

"Are they good people? Your family?"

"They're good guys. I love them to death. But, you're my family."

Time stopped for a second and Keon's heart clenched. He'd been alone with the dragons for so long. So long.

"Shh. Shh, baby. It's okay. Not anymore."

Ice heard him. It was amazing, how Ice heard him.

"I did. I hear your heart." Ice just kissed him, the thoughts in Ice's head happy, despite the circumstances.

All these strangers with their babies.

"You want me to go and check on them?"

"I want to go, too, meet them now that I'm feeling better."

"Sure." Ice climbed out of the big bed and pulled on a pair of pants. Shame. Ice had the finest body in the history of bodies.

"You coming, baby?" Ice grinned like a monkey.

"I suppose I am. I'm less stupid than I was the first time."

"We'll soak in the pool and you'll be right as rain."

"I haven't seen so many people at once in decades, maybe more than a century."

"Well, baby, I would bet you're about to get an eyeful."

He pulled on some soft pants, a gauzy shirt. That way no one would get an eyeful of him but Ice. He liked that, that it was Ice that got to see. Grinning widely, he followed Ice down the cavern, into the wide passage that led to the bathing pools.

The babies were showing off, playing, flying about and swimming. The men were floating, watching it all with awestruck faces.

"They're beautiful, aren't they?" Keon tried for casual, relaxed, and being here with the little ones helped that.

"I can't believe it." The smallest of the team, the one Ice had called Gig, hooted, scattering the babies who'd been nibbling his toes. "They're amazing."

"They are. They're refugees." Orphans.

"Where from?" That was the Cajun, Jack, who looked a lot less awestruck and a lot more… grr.

"All over. Mostly Eastern Europe, but Asia, too."

"So, Asian dragons don't look any different?"

Ice wanted to hear the answer to that, too, he could tell. He forgot Ice hadn't been here all along.

"Cor? Cor, come out?" He sat and held his hand out, waiting

patiently until the shy serpentine boy came to him, sliding through the air like smoke and settling around his shoulders, the world going misty and distant as Cor's magic altered air itself.

Ice hummed. "Look at you! I didn't know if it was just artistic license or what, but there really is a difference, huh? He's beautiful."

"He is. He's shy."

The low song filled the air, gentle, haunting, and he stroked Cor's scales.

The guys all watched, their mouths falling open one by one. It was Gig, though, who stepped forward, eyes huge. "Can I touch him?"

"Hold out your arm. If he's willing, he'll come to you."

Gig nodded. "Sure. Like the wolf I saw at a sanctuary once."

"I've never bonded with a wolf." Keon shrugged, hoping that wasn't bitchy.

Gig held out one arm and Cor's tail carefully slipped out, stroked Gig's fingers. There was a tiny spark, almost as if static electricity had arced between them. Gig's dark brown eyes went wide, his breath hitching. "Oh."

Cor's head tilted, a soft chirruping sound on the air.

"He's amazing. So soft." Gig looked pretty starry-eyed, staring at Cor.

"He's a good boy."

Cor chuckled, fluttered. *Good. Good.*

"He's --" Gig blinked, staring at Cor. "He's talking to me."

Ice looked at Keon, raising a brow. "They're not bonding, are they?"

"They can't be. They can't." Could they? That didn't make sense. How many years had passed since anyone had bonded with his charges? Ice was the first in five decades.

Good? Keon? Good?

He didn't know if Gig was good. Ice said so, but how could Keon be sure?

Gig is a good man. There. Ice just said it again.

This wasn't possible, but there Cor went, reaching for Gig, whispering. No, something was wrong. Keon didn't dare pull Cor back. He could hurt the baby if he broke a bonding, but how could this be?

He looked at Ice, confused, worried. Ice shrugged, waggling his eyebrows like it all made sense. *We're all elementals, baby.*

Elementals.

Oh…

Well, that explained a lot. Like why Cor was cooing at Gig, stroking the lean forearm with his head. Elementals could channel a dragon better than an average human.

"I. Whoa." Gig looked cross-eyed, a little dizzy.

Keon reached out for Damien, desperate for contact. *Did I do something wrong?*

The bond cannot be wrong, beloved.

Promise?

I do not lie to you. Grumpy dragon. *Cor is quite right. These could all be good dragon men.*

At least I have a full house. There were plenty of dragons who needed a bonded, if Damien was right and this was a good thing.

I'm always right!

Of course you are.

Ice snorted. *He should know. He's old, baby. Like, ancient. Wrinkly.*

Old? Damien's growl filled the air and Keon had to chuckle.

He looked at the Gig man, thought at him to see if he could hear everyone, but there was nothing. So, Ice wasn't normal. As normal dragonmen went. That relieved him.

Of course, you could bond and not be a guardian. Guardians heard all the voices, bonded men only their own dragon. He looked at the rest of Ice's guys. The next few days might be weirder than weird.

Ice wrapped one arm around him. *Easy, huh. Breathe.*

There's an army outside, soldiers inside, and you're here with me and that's so new…

I got you. Ice hugged him for a moment, causing everyone but

Gig to stare again.

He held on, needing the support and damn the eyes on them. Ice smelled so good, like cool rain and sex.

"Okay," the big redhead named Shannon glared, arms crossed. "What the fuck is going on?"

"I can hear him in my head," Gig said. "The dragon."

"You can't hear lizards."

"They're not lizards." Humans. They were so quick to make assumptions.

"He's no lizard, man." Gig drew Cor up against his chest and the tiny shy one glowed a warm pink.

Oh, look at that. How could he be worried about that? There were so many little ones and this meant a full life for another.

Chi chirruped and fluttered up to Ice's shoulder. *Not lizard.*

"No, baby. You're a beautiful wee dragon." Keon reached out and Chi wriggled for him, obviously proud.

"This is insane." Jack was a dangerous-looking one, with his scars and eyepatch. He appeared pretty damned pissed off, too, pale, hard lines dug around his mouth. Poor guy. No one liked to have their reality altered.

"That's what Ice said when he came," Keon said.

"Well, he's jumped into the nutso boat."

Ice snorted. "Happily."

"Focus, people." Shannon's voice was a snarl. "Who the fuck are the soldiers out there? What do they want?"

They all turned to look at Shannon, who stood next to the pool, arms akimbo, kinda magnificent in his nudity. Ice had a damned good-looking team.

"They came with Sergei. He tried to steal the younglings," Keon said.

"Tell me about Sergei."

"Shan, you're all naked." Ice waved a hand at Shannon's impressive self. "Can we get dressed before we liaise?"

"Just because you want my bod." Shannon flexed, showing off pale, freckled skin and heavy muscles.

"Ew." Gig finally rejoined them. "Gingers."

Keon leaned into Ice, bemused. "Gingers?"

"Redheads." Gig chuckled. "Shannon is red to the bone."

"I think it's pretty. Shiny." It wasn't Ice's perfect stark hair and bright eyes, but pretty.

They all grinned when Shannon shouted with laughter. "You're all right, lizard man."

"I try." He looked to Ice, who nodded, winked.

"Okay, guys," Ice finally said. "I'll rustle up grub. You get dressed. Gig, check your comms, see if we've had any activity. We'll talk."

"What should I do?" Keon wasn't a soldier.

"I can think of a lot of things." Ice was on a roll, grinning like a monkey.

Damien rumbled softly suddenly, making Keon jump. *They move.*

All the younglings drew around him, surrounding him in a worried mass of wings and tails. They were protecting him, he thought, which was dear.

Ice went into motion immediately, barking orders. "Damien says the Russians are Oscar Mike. Everyone in battle gear. Now."

"Come on, lovelies. Let's move to the back. All of you." He started moving them, herding them deeper into the mountain. "Chi! That means you!"

No. No Ice.

"Now, youngling."

I need you safe, Chi. Go with Keon.

Damien was snarling, huge body lifting into the air through the opening in the old volcano shaft.

Take care, bonded. Take care. Keon sent the thought to Damien quickly.

I promise.

Keon knew with Damien on his side he couldn't lose. With Ice there, too, it was more a worry about how many more people knew where they were, not how many were coming right now.

He got the babies settled, set the four oldest to watching the others. "Stay here. I have to help."

The fluttering of wings and tails made him smile. "I won't be far."

Keon swore.

There was no way he could channel Damien again so soon. It would burn him alive. He had to help Ice, though, even if he had no idea what to do.

Chapter Four

Ice took comfort in how easily his team fell into their old patterns. Everyone was decked out in their gear, Gig monitoring the incoming force on the surveillance setup Chino had put in place.

Damien was staying close to the treeline, on the ground, and was sending Ice images. Dragon recon. Christ, if the governments of the world knew about this…

That was it, though, wasn't it? Someone had sent him, even though Keon had given his whole life so no one knew about the dragons. Ice understood that now. When this was over he would send his team back to DC with word that the weapon had been neutralized. Then he would guard the dragons as Keon did for as long as Chi and the others needed him.

"Shan, how do you want to play this?" Jacques hung back, and Shannon had seemed to step up to take his place as second-in-command.

Ice had no time to figure out what the hell was going on with One-Eyed Jack. They needed to mobilize.

"Let them decide," Shannon said, jerking his chin to the window. "They come in hard, we take them down hard. They're just doing recon? We see what they do from there."

"What if they come back?" Keon frowned, glaring. "What if they come back to hurt the babies?"

"We can't just terminate with prejudice," Jack said, checking the one window in the big door. Ice had to agree. Jack glanced at Keon. "If they're like this Sergei guy you told us about, none of them will get off the mountain. But if they're just kids, foot soldiers, we have to let them go."

Keon didn't say a word, but Ice knew that his lover's first priority was defense. He got it. Where else was the man going to put a dragon stronghold. How strange was it to feel his priorities begin to shift in that direction now, too?

"Maybe I should go talk to them," Keon said.

Jack glared at Keon. "Are you stupid?"

"I don't think so. I'll just tell them to leave."

"And they'll just waltz off?" Shannon frowned, red brows drawing down. "Let us do our job."

Ice reached out, touched Keon's arm. "They'll be safe. I swear to you."

He could hear Keon's thoughts, wild and worried, even as his lover nodded and backed away. *I did this. I brought people here. I was lonely and I brought people here.*

Like Ice wasn't the one who'd peeked into Keon's life and bonded with Chi. Hell, he was the one who'd called in the team. Ice stopped Keon's thoughts with a single barked word. *No.* He stared at Keon, willing him to believe. *They sent me, and more were inevitable. We'll just make sure no more come after this.*

No more. Keon nodded. *No more.*

Keon paced toward the kitchen, intent on the coffee maker.

"That's creepy, man." Shannon stared at him. "You can hear him? Can you hear Gig?"

"Nope. Not unless he talks into my earbud." Ice grinned. "Gig can hear Cor, though."

"No way. Gig?" Shannon peered at their tech guy.

Gig blushed dark. "It's not really words, more like gibberish."

"Cor is really young." Damien would bristle at it being called gibberish, for sure.

"And scared. It's harder for the ones that are different." Keon sounded sure. "Wait for a day or two."

"Okay, y'all. We have movement. A pair of them have split off and are coming into the compound."

Keon's eyes went flat and hard, like someone had turned a switch inside him. Ice wouldn't want to be those men. He stayed calm, though, looking at Chino. "The rest?"

"Surrounding the perimeter."

"Well, then, let's go see what those two want," Shannon said, shouldering an M-4 rifle.

Damien's growl in Ice's head sounded a little like thunder. He couldn't imagine what it sounded like in Keon's.

"What the fuck was that?" Wide-eyed, Chino pulled off his earpiece, shaking his head. Huh. Maybe Damien had done that out loud. Good intimidation tactic. Ice grabbed a weapon and joined Shannon.

There were two soldiers standing outside the compound door, weapons drawn, eyes on the air.

Ice clacked his rifle against the wall, drawing their attention. They might still be able to negotiate. "You boys are trespassing." The soldiers spun, eyes wide. Christ, they were young. Hired kids, then, not true mercs, and not anyone's government ops.

Shannon brought his weapon to bear. "Put down your guns."

One of the kids looked back over his shoulder as if praying help was coming, but the other one dropped the rifle with a clatter. "Sergei."

"Sergei tried to shoot someone. He's dead." Maybe if they knew their leader was gone, they would crumble. When that didn't work, Ice switched to speaking Russian. He wanted to be very clear. This was an occupied mountain.

The kid still holding his rifle barked something he couldn't quite catch, but Ice had a feeling he was calling reinforcements. Shannon moved so fast no one even got to blink, taking the kid down, rifle up one of the guy's nostrils.

The other kid just shook his head, hands up, eyes pure panic.

Ice repeated himself in Russian. Loudly. "Sergei is dead. The rest of you are free to go, as long as you go quiet. If we see anyone else on this mountain, we shoot first. Understood?" *Damien, can I have a nice flame, buddy?*

Where?

Behind them. Between them and their backup. Try not to singe Shan.

Damien's laughter was wicked and more than a bit unnerving, then a shot of fire blasted through, like the world's best flamethrower.

Holy shit, he could see where that would melt rock if Damien really let loose. His team was laughable next to this.

It was short-lived though, and Ice could feel both Damien and Keon's sudden exhaustion.

"Tell the rest of your team that's what will happen to them if they ever speak a word of this place to anyone. Got it?" He picked up the rifle the one kid had dropped and let his own power flow into it, the ice jamming up the trigger and barrel, the metal freezing so fast it shattered.

The boys stared, then broke, running like fools, calling out a retreat.

Shannon grinned. "How long before the next wave comes, and can I play with the next set?" The wind picked up, swirling the dust into patterns at their feet. Shan had a way with the wind.

"They're all yours, man. Depends on how brave or stupid these guys are, huh?"

"Or well-paid. Broke guys run faster." Shannon looked at him. "The fire. That's from a dragon, huh?"

"Biggest one on the mountain, yeah. Takes a lot out of him to do that, though."

"I bet. Where does anything that big sleep?"

"In the cavern. I'll show you." They waited, weapons at the ready, but reinforcements never came. Ice keyed his throat mic. "Gig? Cameras?"

"There's still a few hanging, but the bulk scattered. Where the hell did that fire come from? Also, your buddy's out again, sleeping right here. Boom."

"Damn it. Chino, get out here with Shan and clean up the stragglers. Where the hell is Jack?" Jack was his second-in-command, and usually loud as a flock of geese. He'd been silent for too long.

Gig cleared his throat. "I think, uh, he's having bonding issues, boss."

Ice closed his eyes and counted to ten. "You're shitting me."

"Nope. He clocked out right at the start of the situation. Sitting here with his good eye rolled back in his head."

"You know, this is getting completely out of hand." He'd said himself that his guys were elementals, all good candidates for dragon bonding, but jeez.

Shannon snorted. "You guys are a bunch of pussies."

"I'm coming in." Ice gave Shannon a friendly shove and headed back into the caves so he could set the weapon aside and go to Keon.

Keon was sleeping hard, but there was no fever, just pure exhaustion.

Chino leaned over him. "What the fuck's wrong with him? He a narcoleptic?"

"No. He's drained his reserves. Damien takes a lot out of him and he hasn't had time to recover. Get your ass out there and back Shannon up."

"Bossy old fuck." Chino headed out at a jog.

"Keon." God, he hoped Keon would have some downtime to recover soon. "Hey, babe."

"Ice. Sorry. Sorry. I didn't mean to. He needed."

"Shh." He lifted Keon in his arms, moving him to a chair. "I need to check on Jacques. Jack. Okay? Then I'll take you to bed."

"Okay. I'm good. He's resting. Sleeping."

Lord. He went to Jack, peeling back the lid of the man's one good eye.

Jack's eye moved restlessly, like the man was caught in a dream. He had to wonder which dragon had picked Jack. The most alligator-y one, for sure. He chuckled. Yep. Jacques the Cajun ought to be the most familiar with dragon cousins.

"Is he cool, boss?" Gig sounded worried.

"He's not hurting. He's just gonna have to figure shit out. Help me get him to the bunkroom." The guys could all sleep in the big room he thought of as the guest quarters. The place was like one of those sci-fi things, bigger on the inside.

"Sure. No problem." Gig hollered, "Shannon, get your muscled ass in here!"

Shan jogged in, still toting the M-4. "Looks like the rest cleared out. Gig and Chino are on watch."

"We need to get Jack in a bed, man."

"Shit, get out of the way." Shan handed off the rifle and hoisted Jack into a fireman's carry.

Okay, that was impressive.

IceIceIce. Chi came gallumphing into the room, wings and tail flopping madly. *IceIceIce!* His dragon leapt, wrapped around him.

"Hey, kiddo. It's okay. I'm okay."

No bad mans. No. No no no.

Nope. No more. Ice stroked the soft skin, the leathery wings, soothing.

Chi trilled for him, singing happily, loving him. God, how had he not known this song? He smiled, the tension draining from him. *Let's take Keon to his bed, kiddo.*

Bed. Bed bed bed. He sleeps. Damien sleeps. So deep.

He didn't fall, though. Ice worried about that, like Damien might fall out of the sky when Keon conked out.

No. Keon gives his bonded strength.

Were you watching over me, dear one? His wee protector.

I give you all my heart. All. Chi puffed right up, bared his tiny sharp teeth.

Ice rubbed noses with his little dragon before Shannon came back in sans Jack. "Where do you want this one?" Shan asked, nodding toward Keon.

"Our room. I'll show you." They headed up and up, into the huge room with the new curtained door. He liked the look. Much better than open season on Ice and Keon, which had been the vibe before Ice blocked it off.

"Nice room. Bed?"

"Yeah. Over here." He waved and Shannon gently lowered

Keon down. "Thanks." He stopped Shannon, clapping him on the shoulder. "Check on Jacques again? He's worrying me."

"Will do, boss. Gig and Chino are covering the front."

"Good man. We'll debrief tonight."

"And eat. God. Starving."

"Trust me. We eat good here." He couldn't wait anymore to go to Keon.

He and Chi wrapped around Keon, then the little eyes popped open. *The hatchling. The hatchling.*

Keon woke in a rush. *Where is she?*

I have her. Tatiana's voice was steady. *Serena is crying, biting. She is the one to worry.*

Jacques. Jack. She must be bonding with Jack. Ice shook his head. "I mean Serena. Not the hatchling."

"Oh." Keon looked at him. *Is the hatchling safe?*

I'm almost grown, Keon. Of course. Oh, Lord, the drama. Tatiana could be so snooty, so articulate.

"Is it going to hurt Serena to wait for Jack to wake up?" Ice asked.

"She's nearly grown. If he denies the bond, it'll kill her, but that takes time."

"He won't. He's just stubborn." Ice chuckled, tickled. "She's orange."

"She's gorgeous." Keon was drooping again.

"Jacques will be offended. He'll want her to be camouflage." He helped Keon lie down, got a glass of water.

Keon sucked it down, then settled next to him, leaning hard.

"Tomorrow will be a better day, lover."

"They're gone?"

"Oh, yeah. Shan didn't even get to show off."

"Damien did."

"He so did." He stroked Keon's belly, soothing. "Are you hungry?"

"No. No, I just want to rest." Keon kissed his cheek, and Chi stretched out above them, making proud, happy, in-the-bed-with-Ice sounds.

"Is that okay? That Chi wants to snooze with us?" He was still learning dragon protocol.

"Mmhmm. I sleep with Damien sometimes. He's like a furnace."

Ice had visions of squashed Keon, splattered under a huge sky-elephant.

Keon chuckled. "Good thing he's sleeping."

"He's a little big for sharing in here." Ice moved to massage Keon's hip. "Does me using my ice talent hurt Chi?"

"No. No, you'll learn to help each other when you need to."

"Oh, good. I mean, that trick I pulled I could do in my sleep."

"Now we're wide open inside. It takes a few days to narrow the connection."

Ice blinked. "So did it make you weaker when I did that? Or was it just Damien."

"No. Just Damien. He's so big. You're… like energy."

"That's good." He kissed Keon's brow, which felt feverish. He worked on transferring his inner chill to Keon's body. His lover cooled immediately, fingers twining with his.

Better. Much better. They were all yin and yang.

Fire and ice. Keon's voice was so sure.

Ice nodded before kissing Keon's neck. *That's us, baby. Sleep now.*

He could feel Keon's joy, all the way into dreams. Ice settled with his lover and his dragon and closed his eyes, knowing his guys would wake him if more soldiers came.

His own joy was like a little warm heater in his belly, and that was pretty damned awesome.

Chapter Five

The pain in his head had sent him down to his knees, and from there he'd snapped out of consciousness. Jack wasn't one to hide from his problems. *Non*, he faced them head-on.

A dragon, though, especially a frilly orange girl of a dragon, was another matter. That was who was in his head, after all, whispering, telling him to come bond with her, begging him to make it better.

In his head. Like he was a nutcase who belonged in a nuthatch.

So, Jacques just shorted out, knowing his team needed him and that he was being a big old pussy-man, but completely unable to cope.

He didn't want a dragon. She didn't really want him. The stress of the situation was just getting to everyone, *vraiment?*

Jacques. I need you.

Serena. Her name was Serena, and she was the most beautiful thing he had ever seen. Except she wasn't his, and he couldn't do this. Jack let the sleep take him deeper, hiding far beneath his conscious mind. His whole world was crumbling away beneath his feet. How could a proud man stand for that?

Cowardly or not, he was fucking hiding from now on.

Keon woke up to the sound of distressed dragons. Not an emergency call, or hunger or even fighting. No, this was every dragon in the clutch making little noises of sympathy.

His eyes popped open and he vaulted out of bed. *Damien? Babies? What's wrong?*

Serena hurts. Her man still sleeps. Damien sounded calm as ever. Nothing was ever terribly urgent to a dragon as old as Damien.

Oh. Well, then. He leaned over and poked Ice in the butt. "Go wake the Jack-man up." Enough was enough.

"Ow." Ice rubbed his ass, sleepy voice bleeding into annoyed. "What?"

"Go wake the Jack-man up. Serena hurts. Can't you feel her?"

Ice winced. "Well, I can now. It's like a burning itch all over for her."

"Yep. She's crying. Wake him up. I'll come help." He felt better, awake, ready to stop this nonsense. The bad men were gone, so now they needed to deal with the good ones, he reckoned.

"Gotcha." Ice rolled out of bed, pants hanging so low they gave an amazing view.

Mmm. It was tough, to be a guardian with so many little ones and have those hipbones tempting him.

Serena first. Then Ice's ass. What did Gig say when things all came together? *Boom.*

They headed out, Chi leading the way like a gorgeous blue flag bearer. Chi flourished now that he was bonded, his scales glowing, his little body puffed up with pride.

Keon smiled at Ice. Sweet baby.

Ice took his hand, which made him start. They could do that. Touch whenever they wanted. What a wonderful thing, to have another human there, to have someone to be with.

If you don't wake the human, I will nip him.

"Damien's a little grumpy."

"We're getting there, man. We can't fly."

Jack or Jacques or whoever slept in the big guest bay, curled up tight, arms over his head.

Keon leaned against the wall, staring. "Wake up, Jack."

Jack murmured, turning away from them.

Ice winked at him before going to kick Jack right in the rump. "Stop hiding, you one-eyed coward."

Oh, nice.

Jacques came out of the sheets in a rush, roaring, hands clenched into fists. "What the fuck?"

"Get your ass up and come meet your dragon, you fool."

"I don't have a dragon." Jack crossed his arms over his chest, grimacing.

Keon growled, deep in his chest. "She hurts."

Jack clutched at his head. "Shut up. I can't help."

Serena! Come here!

Hurts. Keon hurts.

Poor Serena. "Fuck this." Ice grabbed Jacques and began dragging him out of the room.

Oh, Keon approved. Pushy, muscle-y and hot. Jack protested, then yelped. Steam rose from Jack's skin, which was fascinating.

"She's amazing. You're hurting her. I won't have it."

"*Merde.*" Jack kept struggling, but it didn't deter Ice one bit. Such a good guardian he was going to be, that Ice.

The older girls shared a den and Tatiana was pacing, her tail swishing as she worried. Serena lay in the darkest corner, her scales so pale she looked transparent, her beautiful eyes closed.

He went to her, pouring love and strength toward her, but it wouldn't matter. "Hey. Hey, I brought you a present."

She looked over at Keon, then closed her eyes. *He thinks I'm ugly. Am I?*

"Of course not. You're perfect."

"He does not think you're ugly," Ice muttered. "He's just being a fucking Cajun. Touch her, Jack. Look into her eyes."

"Well, I only got one eye." Jack flung the words, his voice a snarl. "How can I do that?"

"Are you heartless?" Keon stared at Jack, more angry at him

than he had been at those stupid soldiers. "She was born for you."

"Yeah, then why ain't I stumbled on her before now?" Jack staggered, his dark skin pale and clammy, the bond almost impossible to deny this close. Keon knew how it felt, how difficult it had to be to deny.

Serena stood, swaying gently, looked at Jack for a long moment and then she turned away, slowly leaving the room, a couple of orange scales clattering to the floor.

Beloved.

I know, Damien. I know. His bonded's fury filled his head. This was his home, and Serena was like one of his children. He strode over to Jack and hit the man square in the face with his balled-up fist. "You bastard. I will burn you into ash if she dies. She needs you like air."

"Jacques. Steam. Man, you need to just let go." Ice grabbed a piece of colorful cloth off the floor and used it to staunch the flow of blood from Jack's nose. "You need her, too. The pain in your head will go away."

"Your dude hit me, man," Jacques said, blinking his good eye, his words plaintive.

"I'll do it again."

"Why? Why is this got to be my thing? I was here to help Ice, not be tied down! How am I gonna work with a dragon bond on me?" Jack's accent got so thick Keon could hardly understand.

"Because you're luckier than you could possibly imagine," he snarled.

Ice shook the man, more steam rising where their skin touched.

Serena came back in, nearly white, and she stood before Jacques, trembling. *Not a thing. No man's thing. I will die, yes? No need you.* Her voice dripped with disgust, then she turned to Keon. *No burden.*

Keon went to her, his heart breaking for her. What a fucking day it had been. "You're not a burden, beautiful girl."

She leaned into Keon, just the tiniest bit. Her full weight would have winded him.

"Jack." Ice peered at his team member's face. "Just try. Just look at her. She's this amazing dragon. She's so smart, so damned saucy. You'll love her so much. Just look. If it doesn't work, you can go. I swear."

Ice would never hurt Serena, so he had to believe this would work, right?

Keon stroked her head, the bridge of her nose like he had when she was tiny. "So proud of you, my brave lady."

Hurts, Keon.

"I know. I'm so sorry." What else could he say?

Jack stared right back at Ice, the tension in that whipcord lean body palpable. Then the man very deliberately turned his head and looked at Serena.

Serena looked at Jack, wings curled around her, protecting her heart.

Jack sank to his knees. *"Mon dieu."*

Keon didn't know if that was good or bad. He just held his breath and waited.

Serena stared, head held proud, stiff.

Jack made the most amazing noise before crawling over to lean against Serena's chest. "I'm sorry, *bebe*. I'm so sorry. I didn't know."

Keon looked at Ice, teeth clenched so hard his jaw ached.

Ice nodded, coming to pull him away from Serena. "It'll be all right now, lover. They're acknowledging the bond."

He rested his forehead against Ice's, breathing deeply. "I need to go see Damien." Keon needed to touch his beautiful dragon, hear that all was well.

"You want me to come?" Ice was offering him time alone with dragon. That was sweet, since Ice could hear everything, anyway.

"You help them? Make sure it works?" He was already moving, Damien's call like a siren in his head.

KeonKeonBelovedKeonKeon.

Damien.

He started running, heading up toward Damien's den. His hands shook, the last few days almost too much for him. He needed to lean on his dragon, feel Damien breathe.

The huge heart was bared for him and he snuggled in, immediately lost and found, all at once.

The giant body wrapped around him and held him, closing out the world.

Ice watched Jack and Serena for signs of distress, making sure they seemed to be bonding, not arguing.

That had been fucking insane. Jack was a stubborn fuck. Poor Serena. Her color seeped back into her scales, but it was slow going.

"Jack, go with Serena and have a nap, the both of you." He knew they were chatting mentally. He could hear Serena.

"Nap." Jack didn't even look at him, eye only for Serena now.

"Yep. Buh-bye." Ice rolled his eyes when Serena flipped her tail at him. Silly dragons. Silly humans.

Chi was wrapped around his shoulders, still, so still and unnaturally silent.

My blue boy. Is everything well?

Scared. Serena sick.

Yes. Yes, it was scary. Serena looked like she might keel over on the spot. Keon had never said it, either, but a human who denied the bond would probably go nuts. Jack was usually damned level-headed.

Ice remembered how it had hurt, though, denying Chi. His wee boy rattled his scales. "I know. I was smarter than Jack, though."

Smart. Good Chi.

Very smart, my beautiful one. God, he was starting to talk like

Keon. Like he was a hundred and fifty.

Not yet! One day Chi big! Chi sounded tickled as hell.

"You will be." He stroked Chi's neck. "Should we go find Keon, kiddo?" Serena was scolding Jack, but her mental voice was so sleepy. They were going to do great.

Damien's den. We go there? Oh, that must be a big deal, to sound so awed.

"We'll ask before we go in, huh?" No crispy Chi and Ice.

He sent a curious thought up and got a sleepy, happy call back.

"Woot. We get to nap with the big dogs, kiddo."

Chi chirruped softly, claws tapping on him. Dancing. His adorable dragon. Happiness settled in his belly.

Damien's den was vast, scented with smoke and cinders. Keon was cocooned against Damien's chest, and Ice was honored when the wing pulled him and Chi in too.

"Hey, you two." He addressed Damien as well as Keon. "All looks pretty good out there."

Good. It hurts, to lose them when men leave them.

Keon groaned, snuggled in, as if Damien's words ached.

"I bet it does." They weren't gonna think about that. Not with Gig and Cor cooing at each other and Serena giving Jack hell. Jack was going to regret holding off for a long, long time.

Ice actually grinned, the rest of the tension and adrenaline sliding away.

Chi draped over his side and sang to him, happy and soft, those light wings sliding on his cheeks. Ice spent a moment or two wondering where the heck his life had gone so right and yet so out of control. Then he wrapped his arms around Keon and let himself go to sleep.

Keon woke up, feeling settled and well, the songs from all the young ones ringing. He needed to get up, spend time with the newest hatchling. Tatiana was still young enough that the stress had to be getting to her, and the hatchling needed human handling, too.

He nuzzled Damien, grateful beyond belief for the song of that strong heart.

Most loved. Damien rumbled. *Go play with the baby.*

He nodded, laughing quietly, so he didn't disturb his Ice.

Babies! Babies, let's go swim! Keon wanted to splash.

A thundering herd of dragons in all sizes came down the hallways, the caverns ringing with claws on stone, with flapping wings.

Tatiana had the hatchling and Keon took her, cradling her close before running into the water, laughing hard as they all barreled in. He lifted up on a wave, Tatiana making a huge splash. The hatchling squealed, clinging to his hair. Keon laughed, turning in wide circles, floating and kicking.

Chi came barreling in, torpedoing toward him, almost walking on water. *Keon!*

Beautiful boy!

You mean me? Ice's mental voice was warm, happy. Relaxed.

He looked over, admiring his lover's solid, hard muscles. *You're no boy.*

No? Ice stripped off his pants and waded into the water, coming right to him.

"No." Keon leaned and the hatchling climbed onto Ice.

"Good to know. Hey, baby boy."

The hatchling chittered, only able to offer images, emotions, joy. So damned sweet at that age. Nothing like his old grump.

Don't make me bite you, bonded.

We should go to the lake, Damien. Bathe you. They would do that soon.

Damien's pleasure was immediate, intense, and Ice chuckled, nodded. "You, me, him, a huge brush."

Damien's hum shook the whole cavern. *You would brush my scales, Ice-man?*

"I so would."

"It must be love." Keon winked and ducked as one of the boys sent a huge wave of water.

"Hey, is this a private party? Cor wanted to come be with everyone." Gig came in, Cor riding his shoulder. They were going to need more bedding if these guys were gonna hang around. And they would, since two of them had bonded with dragons.

"Come in. We're having a splash." Keon liked Gig, loved how the man adored Cor.

"Cool." Gig stripped to his undies and slid into the water. "This place is amazeballs."

Amazeballs. Keon didn't think he'd ever heard Cor laugh before, or say such a long word.

"You're gonna teach them bad habits, Gig," Ice murmured.

"Nonsense. I'll bring them into the future." Gig grinned. "Do you see him? He's the most beautiful beast ever."

"Nah, that's Chi." Ice nodded to Chi, who wheeled around just on top of the water.

Keon chuckled. They were all amazing, and his Damien was perfect.

"Hey, are you good at playing lifeguard, Gig?" Gig and Cor were having a ball, Cor chittering at Tatiana, scolding her for shaking her tail.

"I am! Go. Be happy. Shannon and Chino are watching, and we've got this."

"Thanks, man." Ice gave Keon a look that seared him to his toes. "Come on."

"I… Sure." Keon followed his lover, grabbing a towel to wrap around his waist. He didn't know Gig well enough to share his rising hard-on.

Ice pulled him through the compound, to their room, the big bed calling. He hadn't spent so much time there in his whole life, really.

He needed Ice like breathing, wanted to explore every inch

of the hard body. Of course, when he reached for Ice, the man pushed him, sending him tumbling back on the bed. He bounced, a surprised laugh tearing from him. Keon spread his arms and legs, the towel falling open. "What are you gonna do with me?"

Ice hummed, muscling up between his legs on the bed. "Oh, I think I'll make a feast of you, baby. I have some stored up adrenaline still."

He shivered, his cock going from interested to rock-hard. It pointed up toward Ice, who smiled like he'd been presented with his favorite treat.

Then Ice bent and licked a long line down the underside of his cock.

Oh.

Oh, fuck.

His eyes rolled back in his head and his thighs spread wide. Keon needed the release this would bring, needed to let go of the tension.

Ice chuckled, tongue dragging again, slow and steady, and Keon felt every second, every minute movement. His belly quivered, his thighs shaking already. Ice wasn't in any hurry, either, teasing him, lapping at him. Making him crazy. Ice's tongue felt cool, his skin hot, the contrast enough to make his balls draw up hard.

"Mmm. So fast off the gate." Ice tugged them down, weighed them in his palm.

"I can't help it." He simply couldn't. His body was primed for pleasure, and his need was focused on Ice.

"I got you." A tiny wave of cold ran through his sac, which helped back him off just a bit.

"You make me hungry." One leg drew up, his ass sliding on the sheets.

"I love how you taste." Ice sucked the head of his cock right in.

He nearly came up off the bed, hips arching up into Ice's

touch, cock slipping between those lips.

Ice bobbed, licking, sucking, giving him everything he could need.

His fingers tangled in Ice's hair, holding on. He loved how the short strands clung to his fingers, the way Ice moaned when he tugged on it. Ice's tongue slapped on his shaft, making him jump, curl up toward the touch.

Keon wanted to touch Ice, too, but all he could reach was Ice's neck and shoulders, and Ice kept encouraging him back and down.

So he took it all, every bit of loving Ice laid on him, mouth on his cock, hands on his balls, his ass. He called out, moaning and singing to his lover. He petted and praised and finally digressed into sex words and grunts.

That made Ice laugh, tug him in deeper. *Love.*

Oh. Oh, yes. *Love.*

He could hear Ice in his head, talking about the two of them and all the hundreds of years they had to do this, to be together.

It was the best promise, the one he'd never expected. Keon couldn't believe he had Damien, and now Ice. An embarrassment of riches.

No thinking of dragons while I suck you.

He laughed, hard and loud, joy mingling with the pleasure inside him. "Promise. Don't stop."

Never. Ice went all the way down, tongue against the base of his dick, and one finger pushed into his hole, surprising him.

A sharp cry tore from him and he sat up, bearing down and begging for more.

Ice's blue eyes twinkled, pure devil shining out of them. That hard finger slid in deep, then out, not really in time with the sucking. More like a counterpoint.

"Evil." Goddess, Keon adored this man, loved how Ice made him fly.

Absolutely. Ice swallowed around him, the head of his cock hitting the back of Ice's throat, that chill-shock going through him. At the same time, Ice's finger skated across his gland, the touch shocking and perfect enough that he shot, shaking with his orgasm.

Ice took everything he gave, then licked him clean before crawling up next to him, finger slipping free. "Fuck, you're hot when you come."

He chuckled and offered his lips for another kiss. "Well, I am part dragon, hmm?"

"You are. All fierce and wonderful." Ice shared his flavor with him, tongue fucking his lips.

Fierce, wonderful and Ice's.

Balls to bones.

Found

Chapter One

A dragon.

Jesu Cristo. What the hell was old Jack gon' do with an orange, highfalutin, female dragon?

Jacques looked at Serena, who had color back in her scales now that she wasn't wasting away thanks to him ignoring her. He smiled a little. He was gonna love her. That was what he'd do. After that, well, he had no idea.

Serena looked at him, rolled her pretty, multi-faceted eyes. *Silly man.*

"Well, I didn't know dragons existed 'til just these last days," Jack said out loud. Talking inside not out was gonna be odd.

She snorted, but she was pleased, he could tell. Her tail said so, the end flicking his ear. Crazy beast.

He glanced around, realizing the other dragons, and his team, had left them alone. Shit, how much time had passed? Hours? Days? His belly rumbled like Keon's big dragon Damien was in there.

Her head tilted. *Hungry?*

"I am, *cherie.* Starving." He could eat an alligator.

Show you. Serena led the way, making oddly musical noises. Dragon humming.

He could hear the echo of it in his head, too, like she was only being polite making noises out loud. In his mind, she was singing operas. Jack grinned. It did scramble his brain a bit.

"You got to be so girly-girl? Can't you be macho?" He poked her haunch.

She fluttered her eyelashes at him, then bared her teeth, showing a line of long, needle-sharp weapons that would rip his arm off.

"Well, now, that kind of fierce I can get behind."

"Hey." Gig, their Elemental Ops tech guy wandered into the hall, his little Asian dragon clinging to his shoulder. "Shannon is cooking."

"Good. God, I'm starving to death."

The little beast named Cor hid from Jack, face in Gig's throat.

"Don't worry, little dude. I won't let him eat you." Gig stroked Cor's tail.

What a weird turn life had taken.

Keon wandered by, caressing Serena along the way, the odd little man Zen as hell. That crazy hair and mostly naked body still made Jack stare. Lord, he must need to get laid bad if he was jealous that Ice was getting some of that. The scent of bacon and onions hit his nose and sex left his mind in a rush.

"Smells good, Shan." Jack walked into the big kitchen and smiled at the big redheaded soldier who'd been his friend for so long. "No dragon for you, huh?"

"Nope. I'm not hook-up-able."

"Shit, don't say that around here." Ice came in, that white-blond crew cut growing out a little, the smile on Ice's face making Jacques blink. Lord, this place was good for the man.

Shan snorted. "True story. You guys are caught through the…"

Ice cleared his throat. "Little ears."

Shannon blinked, then broke into a huge, booming laugh. "Dude, they're not babies, are they? I mean, they're dragons."

Not a baby. Serena sounded so put out.

"No, but I think Cor might be, sweet girl."

He's tiny. Scared. I am not scared. Grown up.

You're my so brave girl. Jack was amazed at how fast he could go from denial to pure love. He'd been a pure-D idiot, trying to push his dragon away, and his Serena, well, shit. She was the finest young lady he'd ever known. Strong. Brave.

She trilled happily and rubbed her head against his arm, and he scratched her eye ridges, pushing gently.

"Look at you two. You're basking, which, okay, she's a lizard."

Serena was going to bite Shannon. Jack saw the image clearly in his head.

"Shut up, Shan. You just wait. Your turn is coming." Gig sounded so sure.

"Nonsense." Shannon reached into the cooler and pulled out a metric fuck ton of bacon. Jack stared, wondering where that had come from.

"Who does logistics for the dragons?" he asked Ice.

"Keon and some guy in town his family has known for years."

"Some guy? They have all these kids up here and it's some guy?"

Ice's blue eyes narrowed at him. "What are you trying to say, Jack?"

"That we need protection. Real protection for these guys who are trying to come up here and mess with our dragons."

Ice nodded slowly, crossing his arms over his chest to lean back against the counter. "Okay. I can buy that. I guess that means you're staying around, Mister I'm Not a Dragon Man?"

"*Merde*, yes. I won't leave her defenseless."

"No. I know you're not an asshole, Jack." Ice grinned, and it was like old times for a minute. "Much."

"Butthead." He had to smile back, though.

That would look funny. Serena's confusion at the word was clear.

Ice hooted, and Jack remembered someone saying he could hear all the dragons. Lord, Lord, that had to be a bit of noise. Just Serena kept him off balance with her snarky little voice.

Snarky? She poked him hard, one paw pushing at him.

Vraiment. She was so pretty, though.

She leaned against him a bit, carefully snaking her long neck past him and stealing a piece of bacon from the pan.

Shannon stared at her. "Dude. Your girl is a bacon thief."

Serena fluttered her eyelashes, the motion so dramatic.

"Security will be first on our list, then," Shannon said, flipping food onto plates. "Logistics, too, as we'll need more food than Keon has been getting in for just himself."

"Yeah, where's the cash flow coming from, Ice?" Gig asked.

"No idea." Ice shrugged. "I got here, we bonded, you came. Boom."

"Huh. We need to sit down with your boy." Jack wanted to know everything about Keon's set-up.

"Okay. We need to get everyone checked over, get the team all together."

Shannon chuckled. "Assuming you can get out of bed with Keon…"

"Hey!" Ice flushed, and all of them stared at him. Jack didn't even think the man could blush until now.

Okay, this was fun. Genuine all-around fun. He grinned, baring his teeth. "You been busy, for sure."

"You're just jealous, and hush, there are little ears." Ice was obsessed with the dragons hearing things. Surely dragons had sex?

"Listen to the Ops man who became a nursemaid." Chino was the other member of their team, and he came in from running a round of surveillance. "Is that bacon?"

Shannon nodded. "It is. There's enough for everyone."

"Cool. Man, this place is huge. Defensible. Good place. I can see why the dragons stay here."

It's our home. Serena's voice was affronted.

Jack couldn't believe Chino couldn't hear her. Her voice sounded so clear to him.

Ice, though, he smiled at her. "That's right, sweet girl. And we'll keep it safe."

"You know it," Gig agreed. "We need to get some new tech up here, though."

"Keon's not all that technical, guys." Ice looked worried, but it didn't matter to Jack. He needed his soaps.

"So, Ice." Shannon set out bacon and eggs and toast. "Are you gonna have to report in to whoever sent you?"

"I think we'll have to, if for no other reason than I don't want company here."

"Right." Shannon nodded, but let it go.

Jacques looked at Chino, then Shannon. "Are y'all stayin' or getting back to Ops?"

Shannon shook his head. "I won't leave you here."

Chino shrugged. "I can't make any promises, but you guys are my team. We'll see."

That was fair enough.

Are we leaving to go somewhere, Jack-man?

No, honey. He stroked Serena's nose. *No, I just have to know who all is staying from the team, eh? We won't leave but some of them might.*

Serena nuzzled in and settled. *Dieu,* that was all she needed to trust him, his word. He didn't know quite how to take that, because he'd been part of a team, but he'd never been closely bonded to anyone.

He didn't even tend to sleep with the same guy twice.

Jacques grinned. Not like Ice, who had really hooked up with the Keon guy. Like, settling down and making goo-goo faces hooked up. It was vaguely disconcerting and incredibly weird.

Keon himself came wandering in, blinking at them all. "Hey."

Ice held out a hand, and Keon went right to him, smiling brightly.

Tres weird.

Honestly, who was all blinky like that? Jacques wasn't jealous or nothin'. Ice had been far more friendly with their ex-teammate Spider than he ever had been with Jacques. He just thought it was a little embarrassing, like seeing a parent or sibling with their significant other.

Keon needed a mate," Serena said, her mental voice arch. *Sweet and good and right to see him love.*

Such a girl. Jack snorted.

Yes. I am female.

"Okay, so the gang is all here," Shannon said. "Meeting?"

They all agreed and sat down to breakfast and strategy. Looked like Elemental Ops was going from doing high danger missions to dragon tending.

Life was really getting strange.

Life sucked.

A guy fucked up one goddamn assignment, one fucking little mission where a prisoner escapes and kills five people, and said guy gets sent to motherfucking Siberia or Kitch-a-fuckingstan or wherever to hunt lost soldiers in the snow.

Woo-fucking-hoo.

Lane looked at the blinking dot on his handheld that was supposed to lead him to the team's vehicle. Looked at the snow.

The dot.

The snow.

He kept hoping a vehicle would appear. God knew he wasn't a field worker, really. He was an analyst. Risk assessment. Tactical percentages. Shit like that.

So, he'd been wrong about what a werewolf was capable of when it came to steel and tensile strength. So what?

Shit happened.

So, was he supposed to just wait here forever? Lane sighed. Okay. Okay, maybe he needed to be more proactive. Calculate windage or something. He was going to fucking freeze out here. He clicked on his radio, started scanning for signs of life. He hummed a little, the tune "Is There Anyone Out There."

"…you sure, Shan? I mean, seriously?"

"Shut up and string wire, Gig."

Whoa.

Whoa.

People on his radio. English-speaking people. English-speaking people with names he recognized. Okay. So. Now he just needed to triangulate.

Lane cussed under his breath and prayed for a Starbucks to appear in front of him. When he opened his eyes, there was still no latte. Damn. He got moving, his feet freezing.

At least these were the good guys, right? On his side?

Unlikely to shoot him?

He had an ID to show them. A reason to be there. If they'd done their jobs, he wouldn't be in the ice fucking floes. Hell, he was going to quit after this job. Head to New Orleans. Spend a few weeks on the bayou, tossing marshmallows at gators.

Get laid a hundred times.

Lane did a little boogie at the thought. Hoo, yeah. Someone big and hard and rough.

He slowed down as he reached the edge of the forest. What the hell was this? The soaring slope ahead of him had a large compound dug into the side of the mountain. Damn, this was way more than he'd been briefed on.

Lane grabbed his radio again, trying to see if they were still talking on the channel.

"No, you doof. The red wire attaches."

"Don't you two hooligans blow us up."

He swallowed and just went for it. "Home ops to Elemental Ops, over."

There was a long, long silence. Then he heard a totally different voice. "Ops team leader. Identify yourself."

"Uh. This is Lane. They sent me."

"They?" Okay, someone had gone from growly to amused. "Identify."

Shit. He had no idea about communication protocols. "The biggie wows. The home guys. Look, I'm an analyst. I was sent to find you."

"Oh, Jesus fuck. What's your twenty?"

"I'm out here by the trees. There's… some weird compound?"

Lane was as bad at landmarks as he was at radio calls.

"I'll send someone to you."

Thank God. "Sounds good."

"I bet it does. Stay in channel. Out."

Lane shifted from foot to foot, his teeth chattering. How did anyone live here?

This was cold unlike anything he'd ever known. He was from someplace warm. Someplace with hurricanes.

"Hey, man, snap out of it. I could have cut your throat." A giant redhead stood in front of him, seemingly coming out of nowhere.

"Sorry. Sorry. I just…" Where the fuck had this guy come from?

"Come on. An analyst. Christ."

"Yep." That was him. Worthless analyst number 2343572. He followed the guy into the compound, and when they ducked into what looked like a Quonset hut, the warmth flowed into his bones and he moaned.

He wasn't meant to be an icicle.

"I'll get the team leader," the big guy murmured, and disappeared as quick as he'd come, leaving Lane in an office with 1950s furniture, all standard issue. Not military, but definitely government cast-offs.

Weird.

Why on earth would anyone have this all the way out here? He explored, looking around at the thin layer of dust on everything. So no one used the office. Maybe it was a mining operation or something.

"See anything you like?" A burly guy with a near-white crew cut stood just behind him when he whirled around, and he knew this one from his pictures. Ice. Elemental Ops team leader.

"No. I'm supposed to make sure all y'all are alive," Lane said. "You went AWOL."

"No shit?" Ice grinned, looking predatory. "Not here to see why we didn't do what I was sent to do?"

"Who the fuck knows? I'm on official punishment detail. My first and only field assignment and I'm here?" Lane shrugged, hoping his meaning was clear.

"Hey, this is a palace compared to Botswana. Come on." Ice jerked his head and ducked through the door the redhead had slipped out.

Botswana. Christ.

He followed, staying close because it was a fucking warren back in there. The place was -- wow. Carved out of the mountain, obviously heated by volcanic action judging from the steam coming from some of the walls. The warmth, though, suited him to the bone. Lane actually heated up enough to shed his parka by the time Ice led him into a big room that looked like a kitchen. He blinked.

"Want some coffee?"

"Please." *God, yes.*

Ice seemed… genuinely decent. He'd expected all brawn, no brains. Clearly Ice believed Lane's story, which was nice, because it was true. Ice pressed a mug of coffee into his hand.

"Thank you." He drank deep, beginning to shiver, which okay, weird, as he was starting to warm up.

"You're almost blue, man." Ice shook his head. "Jack!"

"What, *cher*?" A voice that was familiar, like home, answered. A Cajun with an accent like slow-dripping honey. Wow.

"I need you to take the analyst to the bathing room. I'll get Shan to make some food." Ice raised a brow at the pirate who came into the kitchen, all dark hair and heavy muscle, one eye covered with a patch.

It was Jean Lafitte made real flesh. His teenaged fantasy brought to life.

Fuck.

The guy looked him over with his one green eye and smiled. The expression managed to be intimidating, not friendly. "Sure, *cher*. Come on, then."

"Where'm I headed, then, y'all?"

"To warm up," Jack the one-eyed wonder said. "You'll see."

Okay. He liked warm. Assuming no one was going to light him on fire. That would hurt. Lane did a momentary risk assessment, studying Jack's body language from behind. Relaxed shoulders, swinging arms, that tight ass moving easily beneath soft shorts.

There was frustration, but zero fear, and no real worry.

Cool.

That was cool.

He took a deep breath, smelling something earthy, a scent he didn't recognize. Lane's head tilted, and he took another breath, deep and hard.

"You part hound, *cher*? Here we go." The world opened up into a huge cavern.

"Water!" He hadn't expected it, the huge bathing pool, steam rising off it, the smaller, curtained areas. The whole place looked like a medieval Turkish bath. "*Dieu*, it's beautiful."

"It is. The water will thaw you out. I just had a bath, so you go on." The Jack guy went and settled on a lounge chair thing set up on the long side of the big pool.

He stripped down to his underwear, and dipped a toe in. Oh. Warm. Perfect. Maybe this wasn't so bad after all. Now he could see why people lived here. If they stayed in the water forever, it would be livable.

Lane closed his eyes and lay back, letting his toes float up.

Okay. Tell the base that everyone was fine, and then hop on a plane to somewhere.

Anywhere.

Someplace warm. This was just a bunch of guys who'd decided to fly off the grid. Go native. Nothing wrong with that, of course. Nothing at all. This was the frozen wasteland of hell, but hey. Everyone had a thing--

The thunder of heavy feet on stone made his eyes pop open, and he stared across the pool and the giant creature rumbling toward him like a freight train. The thing was a cross between a horse and a giant lizard, and it was -- bright orange.

"Lawd, sick gator! Really, really sick gator!" Lane thought he might get eaten.

Jack the one-eyed wonder began laughing. "Oh, *cher*, don't piss her off. That is Serena, the magnificent. She's a dragon."

"A what?" They had lizards called dragons? Lane scrambled out of the water, dripping away.

The dragon spread her wings. Wings. And water went everywhere.

Lane sat down. Bang.

"Yep. You should have seen my reaction. I passed out for a couple days."

"They don't have whatever those are on the bayou."

"No, sir," Jack agreed.

Lane stared. Lord, look at that. It was beautiful. The dragon swam better than it walked, or ran, and came close to peer at him from the water, blinking.

"You are a different kind of gator."

She blew water at him. Out of her nose. Steam came with it.

"She's getting offended, *cher*."

"Sorry. I don't mean offense. She's plumb fine."

"There you go. Now, give her chin a scritch."

"Pardon?" He didn't have any intention of leaving here without a hand.

"She ain't gon' bite you," Jack said. "Much."

"Uh-huh. Is this how y'all get rid of analysts?" He wasn't a chicken-butt, though, no sir, so he reached out and touched her. Her skin felt surprisingly soft, not scaly, and her nose was velvety. Sweet.

"Shit, *cher*, I ain't never met an analyst. I thought y'all was only in movies."

"Yeah, yeah. There's lots of us. Lots." They were replaceable.

"Well, they must be mad at you." The guy finally got up and stripped off, plunging into the water.

"Yeah. Yeah, totally." No looking. Nope. Not even if the guy was built like a brick shit house, all hard muscle, dark hair and scars.

Humina-humina.

"Oh, there's a story there." The dude splashed the big orange gator, chuckling low.

"Where? Oh, you mean me? Nah. I screwed up." Lane watched the man and animal play, utterly bemused.

"How?"

"I didn't understand how damn fast werewolves were."

"No shit? Yeah, we found that out with a mission a while back," Jack said.

"They're totally not dogs."

"Nope. Our boy Spider hooked up with some were-beasties." Jack floated closer.

"Is it safe? To get in again?"

"Sure it is." Jack winked his one good eye. "No more coming because you're a stranger."

He had absolutely no intention of coming. Going. He was fixin' to go. Well, hopefully.

"Dragons, I mean. They won't come down until they get the all clear that you're safe."

"There's more?" That was a lot of lizards.

"There are way more, *cher*. Come on and get warm."

He slipped back into the water, hiding his erection with his hand. How embarrassing. *Hi, I'm here to see why you fucked up because I fucked up and now I want to fuck.* He was an idiot. At least there were shadows and the man only had one eye, right? Maybe he couldn't tell Lane was all het up.

"No need to be ashamed of that piece of rope, *cher*. It's a fine thing."

Oh. Oh, good Lord. So much for Jack not noticing. "Sorry. I just... Bodies are weird things."

"You're not into men?" Jack stopped a few feet away, the casual floating not so casual now. "You better say so now, *cher*."

"What?" He was totally into dick. Happily. Hell, he had a

rainbow inked into his chest.

"Well, you're acting like you're all ashamed." Jack was dangerous. All of a sudden that became very clear.

"Not ashamed, I usually don't just spring wood at the sight of a hot son of a bitch."

Jack moved another foot closer, close enough to reach up and touch his cheek. "Well, now, you've had a long day."

Electricity hit him, surged through his body and he moaned, the connection fierce, intense. He'd never felt anything like that. Steam began to rise around, the dragon making a grumpy noise and splashing out of the pool and out of sight as if to give them some alone time.

Lane pushed close, slamming them together, completely lost in the song that was Jack.

Jack's hands slid under his ass, and Jack kissed him, mouth on his, hot and damp. Oh, hell yes. The steam surrounded them and he groaned, tongue pushing against Jack's. So long. It had been so very long.

The kiss was gonna burn him to the ground. God, that was good, the slide of lips and tongue, the way Jack pushed against his cock with one leg.

Lane took it, rocking down, energy soaring inside him with the pressure.

"Yeah. Oh, *cher*, I could hear how bad you needed, could feel it," Jack said between nibbling his skin.

"Please. Please, yes." Hear him. Touch. Lick. Fuck. All the things. He couldn't believe how hungry he was, how Jack's touch made him shake. He didn't even know this man.

It didn't matter, the touch was like fire.

Lane humped up, his hips rocking, his breath coming in shallow pants.

"Hungry man." Jack bit his lip, tugged, and he almost screamed.

Lane did cry out when Jack pushed back and tugged his underwear off. Then that huge hand wrapped around his cock and he arched, head hitting the water.

He didn't have to beg, or push or anything. Jack stroked him, thumb pushing at his slit.

The energy built and built, rocketing between his nerves. He didn't know what to do, didn't know how to give anything back. He was going to explode, combust.

"You're just overdue for an orgasm, *cher*."

"Help me." The only thing in the entire world was this one-eyed Jack.

"Uh-huh. Feel me, *cher*. Feel my hand." Jack jerked harder, making his balls draw up.

Lane bowed up, the surge of energy releasing in a huge wave as he shot. Lane gritted his teeth on a shout, his body swaying, sawing back and forth.

There was a clap of thunder, then rain began to fall, dissipating the steam.

"Shit!" Jack laughed out loud, holding him close, protecting him.

"Sorry. Sorry, I can't help it, *douce*," Lane said, his own Cajun accent coming to the fore.

"You doin' that, huh? Come on, out of the water. Cold rain ain't helpin' no one." Jack towed him out of the pool like a dead river barge.

"Dude, it's raining in the cave." Gig was there suddenly, blinking. "That is made of win."

"Cannonball!" The big redhead rushed past them, slamming into the water.

Jack held him, kept him close, protected. What an odd feeling. He'd been on his own for so long.

"Shh. You got this, *cher*. You got this."

"I do." When he glanced up, his eyes widened. "That's -- are all those dragons?"

"Yep. They're babies, most of them. Neat, huh?"

"Babies?" They looked huge. Some of them. A lot of the staring eyes belonged to little ones no bigger than iguanas.

"Look at all the colors."

"Aren't they pretty?"

They were absolutely stunning. He loved how they all had a bright shade all their own, how their eyes glowed.

Especially lovely was the tiny one. The teeny, tiny emerald green one. "Oh. Oh, look at you."

He reached out and the wee thing curled into his palm, tail circling his wrist.

Lane looked into its eyes, a shiny silver and blue, and he was lost. Utterly lost.

Chapter Two

A w, hell," Gig said. "We got another one. Someone needs to get Keon."

Shannon's nose wrinkled. "This is ridiculous."

"You're only saying that because they all rejected you, dude," Gig teased.

Jack snorted. "Y'all be good." He patted Lane's shoulder, wishing he'd gotten his orgasm in before it rained. Next time, he'd go first.

Lane was staring, eyes wide and fastened on the dragon.

"What's its name, honey?" Jack asked, knowing Lane would know by now.

"Geri. Her name is Geri. How do I know her name is... *Mon dieu*, you're beautiful, bebe girl."

Little Geri curled up against the crook of Lane's arm, burped, and fell asleep. Bang. Such a baby.

"She... she's tiny. Like a chameleon." Lane looked stunned.

"Don't make her bite you, *cher*." Jack grinned, knowing his one good eye had to be twinkling. Lane was a good bit smarter than him, just letting the wee beast in so easily.

"She wouldn't do that to me." Lane stroked her, the touch bothering the little dragon not a bit.

"No? She's a baby. When she gets to be my Serena's size, it hurts."

"What does?"

"The biting." Jack snapped his teeth together.

He saw the way Lane shivered, the way those eyes -- as gray

as a stormy day -- heated.

Oh, now, that was something. That hot little man was looking at him as if he'd hung the moon. Sweet as hell. His cock reminded him he didn't get to come. Damn. Maybe he could soon.

He'd love to feel Lane's lips wrapped around his cock, pulling at him. Hell, he'd love to have a hand job right now. He might have to settle for his own, though.

Lane's hand was full right now.

Jacques grumbled a bit in patois, his mood plummeting.

"Is there… Do you have a place, *douce*? To go rest?"

He looked at Lane, nodding. "I know where we can go, yeah."

"Where should this wee one sleep?"

"Serena will help with that, huh, baby girl? They have to stay close to us for a bit."

I will help. You're all silly for this an-a-leest.

His girl was a little snarky, her inner voice almost like a teenager. Jack grinned.

Serena reached for the little one, and Lane smiled at her. "Please be gentle, she's only tiny."

A loud snort sounded, and Jack laughed out loud. "She been mothering the babies a while now, *cher*. Come with me."

Lane let Serena take Geri, which was good because Jack was going to lose his shit if he didn't get at that fine little body, especially now that he knew Lane wanted it as bad as he did.

He grabbed Lane's hand and started towing the man toward the more private end of the cave, where the sleeping area was. He and the boys would have to make it more comfy for them to stay soon.

Somewhere more permanent and a little less hard.

Oh, hard.

He knew all about hard. His dick ached, pressing against the pants he'd hastily pulled on, and he stopped, yanking Lane up against him.

"Yes." Another shot of electricity seemed to hit the little

Cajun and his laugh filled the air.

Wasn't that fine?

Jack took that mouth in a deep kiss. Oh, fuck, yes.

Lane tore at his fly, tugging at his pants, trying to get at his dick. Jack let those clever fingers dig in and pull him out, let Lane moan and tug at him. The man obviously appreciated a fine cock, because Lane groaned, stroked him from base to tip.

Gritting his teeth, he pushed into the touches. "More, *cher*."

"*Oui. Oui*, more." Lane's hand had none of the limp-wristed softness he was expecting. No, the grip felt strong, steady, the friction pulling at his balls. He wanted to wiggle, to twist, but he stayed still, let Lane work for it.

There was no way this one would disappoint, either. Lane went down on his knees, cheek rubbing Jack's cock.

Oh, fuck yeah. He wanted that mouth, wrapped around him and sucking hard. He looked down, watching, his depth perception making it less than perfect, but Jack didn't care.

He knew how to feel, for sure. Every single touch. That hot mouth worked him, Lane pulling back to lick the head of his dick, then pushing down to suck at the base. That was what he needed, the hunger, the want.

The suction. *Jesu*, that felt good.

Lane's moan was deep, low, vibrating all around his cock. He stroked Lane's thick hair, encouraging. He wanted to show how good it was, how much pleasure Lane gave him. Lane looked up at him, sucking hard, moaning around his prick.

Sweet man. Jack stroked the back of Lane's neck and Lane took more, swallowing around his prick. Fuck. He was going to lose it any moment, just blow like crazy.

One hand cupped his balls, rolled them, pushed at them.

Lane was ready for him to come, too.

He groaned, started fucking Lane's lips, pushing in, over and over. His hips rocked back and forth, his breath coming in harsh pants and Lane took him, took it all. When Lane's front teeth scraped the head of his dick the tiniest bit it was all over. Boom.

Jack came so hard he saw stars.

Lane swallowed over and over, pulling and sucking against his sensitive cock.

"Damn, *cher*. That was good." The way Lane hummed around his cock made him bare his teeth. This one was special, For real. "Come lie with old Jacques, *cher*."

Lane looked at him, nuzzled his belly. "Yeah?"

"Yes." He pulled Lane up to standing, then took a kiss. "You look worn out."

"Been a long few days."

"I bet." He half-carried Lane to the pile of pillows and blankets. "What's an analyst gonna do up here, anyway?"

"Find y'all. I did it, too." And Lane sounded damn pleased.

"Well, all you had to do was climb the mountain." Jack shook his head. "What's your talent, *cher*?"

"I don't have one."

Oh, nonsense. This *douce* had to be like him and the rest of the team, having some sort of elemental talent. That little dragon said so just by bonding with him.

Hell, he'd seen the rain falling in the cave, felt the jolt of electricity that shot through him. His own talent was steam, not rain.

So, Jack waited. Staring.

"I can't control it. I just gather energy and then it goes off."

"What does?" Jack tilted his head, trying to understand.

Lane shrugged. "It gets bigger and bigger and then, boom. Something happens."

"Like the rain?"

Lane's cheeks were a deep, dark red, but Jacques got a nod.

"Well, we can work with that. We got to figure what to do with the team, after all."

Lane nodded, obviously exhausted, confused.

"Come on, *cher*. We'll sleep. Serena and your Geri will come."

"Will they? I... I'm feeling very confused."

"You need to rest, let the bond form." Jack eased the sweet

one down. "Trust me. I know."

He knew better than anyone. He'd been the fool to deny his dragon.

Serena, beauty. Bring the wee one with you and we'll nap?

Naps are good. He heard her galumph down the hall. Her nails clicked and clacked, the sound oddly comforting.

Lane looked like he might freak out a little until little Geri scampered off Serena's back and curled against Lane's chest.

"Oh, *petit.* There you are."

"They do make things better, *oui?*"

Lane nodded, leaned against him as he rested against Serena. Serena grumbled about having to share her bunk with the *bebe,* but he shushed her easily. She was ready to be with him for a bit, sharing space. This was all new to her, too, and things had been so fast, so strange.

Lane's fingers moved constantly, petting and stroking. Tactile man. Jack liked that. *Cristo,* his life had been hijacked for good.

How on earth had he found this world?

Singing. The world was filled with song.

Lane smiled, searched for the source of the music, straining to hear. Something tickled his wrist, something so soft and gentle. A soft coo sounded, and then the song continued, got louder.

Geri. He glanced down at the tiny dragon curled around him.

"Hey, there. You singing to me?" Lane asked.

Geri's crystal-colored eyes shone up at him, and the song intensified. What a lovely sound. Lane figured the wee one was happy, right? The song seemed joyful. The noise made him glad deep inside, too. He grinned, carefully stretching so he didn't dislodge his dragon.

His back rubbed against warm bare skin and a heavy hand wrapped around his belly, keeping him close.

Oh, hello. One-Eyed Jack. Yum.

Jack kissed the back of his neck. "*Bonjour, cher.*"

"*Bonjour.*" He leaned, making the offer for another kiss.

Jack hummed before taking his mouth, bending him back against one broad shoulder. The kiss started slowly and he heard a harrumph before the wee one was eased off his chest.

Jack chuckled. "Am not."

"Are not what?"

"She thinks we're perverse."

"She talks to you?"

"*Oui, cher.* She's older than your girl, though. It will come."

"Oh. Oh, wow. Yes, please." He wanted to hear Geri speak. In his mind, out loud, he didn't care much.

"Come on, then. It's time to feed them. Then we can get perverse."

"What do they eat?" What exactly was this place? Some kind of dragon clearing house? It was bigger than he thought.

"Hot dogs. Fish. Bologna." Jack chuckled when Geri flapped and chittered.

"She knows that, doesn't she?" God, the cute factor was through the roof. He was utterly besotted with Geri and Jack, both.

"Looks like. Serena liked turkey."

"Meat eaters, then?"

"They'll eat fruit. Twinkies. I got no idea what's good for them. We need to ask Keon." Jack blinked that one good eye.

"Have I met him?" He didn't remember that name…

"Little guy. Crazy hair. Like that anime, no?"

Lane nodded, but he really didn't remember at all.

"I'll introduce you again. He's the big dragonkeeper or something. Ow!" Jack jumped half a foot.

"Jack?" Little tingles of energy came running to him, drawn from everywhere, his body ready to help Jack if real distress was imminent.

"Serena bit me. Come on, *cher*, 'fore she gets worse."

"Sure." He felt each little spark, like a tiny burn.

"You okay?" Jack got up close, peering at him.

"Am I?" He reached out, put his hand on Jack's arm and the energy transferred with a pop.

"You shocked me." Jack started, then grinned. "Oooeee."

"Thanks. It was building up." Burning a bit.

Jack tilted his head as if he was a puppy hearing a whistle. "Man, we can use someone like you. Good thing you'll be sticking around."

"I will? Is it always this cold here? Do you think they'll let me transfer? Or is it make me transfer…"

"I don't know if it's this cold all the time, but you can't just go and take Geri."

"Well, I won't leave her." Lane didn't even know what the hell she was all about, but she needed him. He needed her.

"You can't." Jack said it cheerfully, sliding out of the bed to tug on some pants.

Lane didn't know about that, but he did know she was the most beautiful girl he'd ever seen. "Do you know where my clothes ended up?"

"Nope." Jacques pulled out a pair of sweats for him. "These ought to do you well enough."

"Soft. Thank you." They floated on him like a warm fuzzy jellyfish. That was awesome. He looked down, chuckling.

"You're damn near as wee as your dragon."

Lane rubbed gently along Geri's spine. "Did you hear him? Maligning us?"

Geri made the most amazing noise, a little trill he thought was a "yes." Perfect girl.

"She heard you, man. We're not small, we're fun-sized," Lane said.

"Uh-huh. Tiny. Right, Serena?"

The big orange dragon made a noise, too. Complete agreement. They were so expressive these dragons. Not like sick gators at all.

"Nonsense. We're fierce. Show them your teeth, baby doll."

Tiny Geri growled fiercely, baring baby teeth.

Jack burst out laughing. "Oh, *cher*, you should see Damien. He's the biggest one of the dragons."

"Is he? How big is biggest?" Did he want to know?

Geri sat up on his arm and spread her wings, puffing up as big as she could.

Jack shook his head. "You have to see it to believe it."

"Wow. I can't wait."

Serena led the way out into the hall. "Well, you follow us," Jack said. "If you get lost, Geri can show you the way."

"I'm coming. This place is… Lord have mercy." It was a warren. Hell, Lane didn't know how the mountain could hold with all the holes in it. The place had to look like a honeycomb on a satellite image.

Warm, though.

And weirdly homey.

The halls echoed with voices and strange sounds, and he smelled food as soon as they got close to what he thought he remembered was a kitchen.

Oh, man, he was hungry, possibly starving. His belly rumbled and Geri hissed.

"I'll get you something, baby girl. I swear."

"Ah, hey, baby girl." A guy about his size with crazy black hair and bright eyes smiled at Serena when they walked in. "Feeding time."

This must be the Keon he didn't remember.

"She's hungry. Like grr-arrgh." He held out his hand. "Lane. Lane Beauchamp."

"Keon. I was a little out of it when you showed up. Been a busy week."

Ice, who Lane totally remembered, snorted. The man was intimidating. Big, muscled, icy-blond. He'd read Ice's file. The man was… fierce.

Jacques he knew way less about. Well, that wasn't exactly

true, was it? He knew a lot about how the man tasted. Lane grinned, then found everyone staring at him.

"Sorry. What?"

"What would you like to eat, man? We got ham sandwiches and stuff, omelets." Keon winked.

"I want to make sure she eats first, please. She's so wee."

Keon's whole demeanor softened. "She's a doll."

"She's perfect." His dragon. Her song filled him.

"She is. Let's get her some cream, hmm?"

He stroked her head. "She likes cream?"

"She does. It's easy on her wee belly. She likes eggs, too." Keon was going to be a fount of knowledge, he could tell.

"Well, let's feed her!" Lane wanted to share everything with Geri.

Keon found him a tiny saucer, filled it with cream, and the wee beast began to vibrate, purring for it, just like a kitty. Lane put her down on the table Keon pointed him toward, and she went for the cream. Bang.

Oh, God. God, that was something else. He watched, fascinated. Not a dainty eater his girl. Greedy gut. Her song backed off from a cry to a happy hum.

"Oh, there. There, better." Lane grinned at Keon. "She thought she was starving."

"She's so young. She'll get to where she only needs to eat once a day after a while." Keon beamed at him. "I can't believe one so tiny bonded. That's amazing."

Lane blinked, then smiled back because Keon was impossible not to like. "Eventually someone will explain what all this means, right?"

"Yes. As soon as I figure it out, I'll let you know."

Jack hooted. "I hear that, Keon. This is all a big pile of--"

Ice cut Jack off. "You trying to piss off your girl again, Steam?" Ice asked, using his team nickname.

Serena blew her lips at Ice, scales rattling.

Lane remained amazed at the dragons. So smart and

wonderful. He could see why Ice's team hadn't destroyed them or called in the government bureaucrats to make them into weapons. He chewed his lips trying to figure out what he would do with his report. It wasn't like he could betray them. That was… unthinkable.

Somehow he had to make the bosses decide this wasn't a viable project. He couldn't say anything that would cause suspicion or that would be hinky.

"What are you thinkin' about so hard, *cher*?" Jacques sat next to where Lane stood and then pulled Lane down on his lap.

"What to tell the home office so that no one finds us."

"Oh, Ice been wrangling with that, too."

"We'll figure something out."

All of a sudden he realized everyone was watching them. Not unkindly, just… staring.

Jacques wrapped an arm around him, holding on. "Ignore them. They's buttheads."

"Hey, we're just not used to seeing anyone but Ice getting it on." The big redhead, Shannon, maybe? He came in and slapped Jack on the back.

Christ on a crutch, he never just hooked up. Never. This whole situation was nuts. A dragon, a new lover. Lane felt like gibbering.

"Shh, *cher*. Shh." Jacques' hand moved up and down his back, soothing him. "All a bit much, huh?"

"Yeah. Yeah, *douce*. I… I feel like I'm down the rabbit hole."

"Oh, hey, you're doing great," Shannon said. "Jack went all catatonic for two days."

"Fucker!" Jack swatted at Shannon, and Lane started laughing. "Unlike you, *cher*, I tried to deny the dragon-bond," Jack told Lane.

"Why?" He couldn't imagine. Of course, Serena was vastly more intimidating than his tiny Geri. And orange. Which was not as manly as emerald green.

"Because I didn't want to be tied down." Jack made this

noise, half-pained, half-funny. "I was so damned stupid."

He wasn't so sure about that. Yesterday he was freezing his ass off, today he was bonded to a dragon and fucking a Cajun. Lane wasn't complaining, but sudden life changes could be a bit scary. Listen to him with the logic and shit.

Geri burped and fell over on the table, fast asleep. Oh, God, she was the cutest.

Ice handed him a bacon sandwich. "Eat."

"Thanks, man." Jack tried a smile, and got one back. Okay, so Ice was scary, but hot.

Jack growled softly and he offered a bite, but Ice was the one that stared Jack down.

"Oh, I have no intention of getting into a pissing contest with you, man," Ice murmured.

"No? Good. This one is mine." Jack held him close.

Ice laughed, the sound warm, tickled. "Sure, man. Have at it."

Lane grinned like a fool, feeling warmth bloom in his belly at being the object of Jack's jealousy. "I'm right here, you know."

Jack nodded. "I'm aware, *cher.*"

"Be good," Keon murmured. "There are wee ones about."

"Mine is asleep," Lane pointed out.

"Mine is eating like a horse." Jack rose, lifting him. "We'll be back in a bit."

He squealed a little, but his cock responded to the show of strength like a champ, rising in Jack's borrowed sweats. By the time they got back to Jack's sleeping area, the head was poking out of the waistband.

"Mmm. Is that for me, *cher?*" Jack asked.

"It's not for Ice."

"Don't make me beat your ass." Jack paused to stare at him. "Unless you're into that, and then I'm willing."

"Jack!"

"What?" Jack kissed his mouth, hard. "I want to do bad things with you, *cher.* Bad, bad things."

His cock went from interested to diamond-hard, as if Jacques' voice was a caress in its own right. The man made him right stupid with need.

"My turn to taste you, Lane." Jack lowered him to the bed, stripping off his pants.

Lane arched, moaning deep in his chest, the sound echoing off the stone walls around them. He wanted Jack's mouth on him so badly it hurt deep in his belly.

Jack cupped his cock, his balls, surrounding them in that huge hand. The calluses there reminded him how Jack worked with his hands, a dangerous man. That fact only made his desire stronger. He spread wide, pushing into the touch and making a clear offer.

Chuckling, Jack stroked him up and down a few more times, bending to tease one of Lane's nipples with his tongue.

His pecs tensed, his nipple aching and eager for more. Honestly, he'd hardly ever considered his nipples before. He was considering them now. Rather intensely, especially when Jack pinched the other one. Lane sucked in a deep breath, lungs filling as he grabbed Jack's shoulders.

Jack chuckled, sliding down his body to spread his legs and slip between them. Then that hot mouth landed on him, lips closing around the tip of Lane's cock.

He was expecting Jack to take more, and the pressure on his cock was surprisingly sharp. Lane panted, his hips rocking, his hands opening and closing. Jack's tongue slapped the tip, the slit stinging at the sweet pop.

God, he hadn't ever played like this. Sex was quick. Hidden. Jack was just making him crazed. One leg drew up, his entire body trying to spread, to process information. He shook a little when Jack went all the way down, sucking him to the base of his cock. Lane swallowed, his chin drawing in, his legs shaking.

Jack reached between his legs to roll his balls in their sac, slow and easy. That pressure was delicious, maddening and perfect, all at once. He panted, his body on high alert.

"Gon' make you scream, *cher*." Oh, such good promises Jack made him.

"Please. Please, I want to feel."

"Everything." Jack took him in again, swallowing hard around his prick.

"Fuck!" He arched back, his hips pumping. Huge hands wrapped around his hips, stilling him.

Jack was in control. Period.

His muscles clenched, his balls drawing up. He was so close, his belly quivering, and Jack held him down, thumbs rubbing hard against his skin. That mouth never let up, Jack sucking and licking, taking him deep over and over. When his cock hit the back of Jack's throat, Lane knew it was all over.

He really did scream when he came. He'd swear Jack was laughing around his cock at him. Lane would show Jack a thing or two. As soon as he found his brain. Of course, Jack was still sucking, still pulling at his sensitive cock.

"Jack." He tugged at Jack's shoulders. "Please. Need to touch you."

Jack bit and nuzzled all the way up, teasing his skin. Goosebumps rose on his flesh, and Lane shivered, his nipples hard as nails.

"Want to fuck you now, *cher*." Jack waggled the eyebrow above his good eye.

He reached up, touched the eye patch, traced it.

"Don't want to ruin the mood, Lane." Jacques smiled for him. "If you want to see, though, it ain't nasty."

"I want to see. I want to know everything." How he could be so involved with this man so fast was a mystery, but he really didn't care to solve it.

"All right, then." Jack took off the patch, and all there was behind it was scars, a patch of skin that had been pulled across the socket. He touched it gently, then pushed into a hard, needy kiss.

Jack gave him what he craved, lips pressing his, tongue

pushing in, tasting him. They held on to each other, squeezing tight, deep moans filling the air.

He felt Jack's cock, hard against his belly, wet at the tip. His hips rolled up, rocking up into Jack, making a clear offer.

"Need to find some oil, *cher.*"

Oil. Oil. Where? "Is there any?" Lane asked.

"I should have something in my kit bag."

"Where?"

"Hell if I know." Jack laughed out loud, the sound echoing off the walls. "Let me look."

He opened his arms and let go, grudgingly. Jack moved away from him, rummaging, ass hard and round and perfect and pointing back toward him.

He moaned, lips parted, as he followed that fine fucking body without thinking.

"Where you goin', *cher?*" Jack turned to glance at him.

"Going?" Lane wrapped his hand around his cock, tugging lightly.

"You were moving. I need you right there."

"I'm not going anywhere. I was admiring."

"Oh. Well, then, that's okay." Jack went back to digging and crowed a few moments later. "Here we go."

Lane applauded, tickled, the sound surprisingly loud.

"I know, huh?" Jack looked happy, his smile huge.

"It echoes in here." The babies couldn't hear them, right?

"Oh, Lord, honey. It's a cave." Jack flopped next to him, cock bouncing.

Lane nodded, reached for that club of a prick. "Uh-huh."

"Here. I found some rubbers, too." Jack had the best kit bag.

"Magical." Lane pumped Jack's dick, watching it swell.

"Me? Nah. I'm in Ops. We're more prepared than them kid scouts."

He wasn't. He was here because he was a fuckup. Jack didn't look at him like he was an idiot, though. Jack was looking at him like he was the hottest man on earth. That really gave him a shot in the arm, and it made his dick nice and hard again.

"Mmm." Jack reached for him, cupping his package, fingers working him.

"No. I mean, yes, but the oil, Jack. Please." He needed to feel Jack inside him.

"Needy little man." The words heated him, all through.

"I am. You promised." Lane touched Jack's cock, just the tip.

"I meant every fucking word, *bebe*."

"Good." Feeling super brave, Lane grabbed the lube and got it open so he could start to prepare, slick his fingers. God, he felt daring. Like a porn star, especially the way Jack moaned and licked his lips. He gave it his best, hips rolling, body on high alert. He focused on Jack's responses, wanting to make this good for them both.

Jack finally pounced on him, cock covered in a rubber, and grabbed the lube. "Now, *bebe*. I can't wait."

"Now. Now works for me." Lane spread wide.

"Good." Jack slicked up that prodigious cock and pushed between Lane's legs, setting the tip against his hole. He didn't give either of them a chance to freak out or worry or anything.

He simply bore down and took Jack in.

Jack pushed right inside him, as if he belonged there, fitting better than Lane would have thought possible. His eyes rolled up in his head, energy already building along his skin. He felt it like sparks, like steam rising inside him, filling every inch of him.

Oh, that was warm. Good. Jack was so hot to the touch, his skin on fire for Lane.

He left desperate, sucking kisses along Jack's jawline, his muscles closing tight around Jack's dick.

"You ready for me to move, *cher*?"

"Please. Need you to." He grabbed Jack's shoulders.

Jack nodded, gritting his teeth, and began to move slowly. He could feel every inch, spreading and stretching him. His body tried to clamp down, then open up, the invasion pushing him to the limit.

A sound slid out of him, too huge to hold in.

"Uh-huh. Let me hear you."

Lane wasn't sure he had a choice. There was no space for sounds to hide inside him.

"Love that. Love to hear you beg and moan." Jack got moving fast, and Lane nodded, not even certain what he agreed to.

It didn't matter. Right now, right here, he would give Jack anything so long as it didn't stop. Jack fucked like a well-oiled machine, face set in hard lines, that one green eye blazing at him. Lane's teeth dug into his bottom lip, the sting keeping him in control. He jerked, riding Jack's cock, meeting every thrust with one of his own.

"Good. Good, take me." Jack was all grunts and growls.

"All of you," Lane agreed. "Big. Feels amazing."

He loved the way Jack slammed against him, rattling his bones. The act made him grunt, gasp, his legs coming up to wrap around Jack's sturdy body.

"Please. More."

Jack gave him more, that thick cock pushing against him. He could barely breathe, could hardly see. He'd come once; he couldn't imagine how bad Jack needed to come. Still the man kept going, kept fucking him.

His ass burned, his muscles jumping under his skin. That was when he started begging. Lane had never needed anything so much.

"Gonna, *cher*. So soon."

"Please. Now." He fisted his cock, bore down hard.

Jack shouted for him, a musical sound that held no words. His ass was so damned full and there wasn't an inch of him that wasn't awake, so alive.

When Jack's orgasm faded, those hard fingers closed around him, pulling at his cock. "Yeah." His shoulders rolled up and he rocked down.

"Come on, *cher*. Come on." Jack was generous, giving him more friction, more perfect need.

Lane did. He came on himself. He came on Jack. He came all over the damned place. Two orgasms in less than hour. That might be a record. Okay, it definitely was for him. "Mmm. S'good," he murmured.

"It is." There was no mistaking the satisfaction in Jack's voice.

They had no time to bask, though, because the thunder of dragon feet on stone sounded, Serena careening into their space, little Geri on her back.

"What's wrong?" Jack pushed back, grabbed his pants, and Lane did the same.

Geri gibbered at him, sounding panicked as hell. She swarmed up Lane's arm just as Jack's whole team burst into the room. He backed up, protecting her baby body.

Serena rose up, hissing, wings spreading.

"You bloody bastard!" Shannon hollered, hands clenched into huge fists. Someone was about to try to tear his head off. How much would that suck?

Chapter Three

L ane looked behind him. "Who? Me?"

"What's all this, then?" Jack asked, seemingly unfazed.

"He's a fucker. He's carrying a beacon, bringing them right to us!"

"Who did?" How could he have done that? Lane didn't know anything about a beacon. He'd had his handheld radio, but they'd taken that from him when he'd arrived.

"You did, you little shit." That came from the Gig guy, the one who did all the electronic stuff. The room was beginning to smell like brimstone and rain.

"I didn't!" Lane backed up, keeping Geri protected. He hadn't done anything wrong. Nothing. "I wouldn't know a beacon if it bit me on the ass. I'm an analyst."

"Now, y'all, does he seem dangerous?" Jack took his arm, the one not holding Geri. "Someone is using him."

"He's a traitor!" Shannon growled.

"Nonsense. Geri loves him." That was Kim… Kevin… Keon?

Nice to know someone was on his side.

"Are you suggesting that having a dragon want to hump you makes you a good person? Seriously? You have met Jack, right?"

"Hey!" Jacques did look offended now, made even more intense by the lack of eye patch. "He's on our side, okay? We're all wasting time we should be using to figure out if anyone gon' come after us."

"I want him contained until we're sure. It's the most logical answer." Ice winced, then growled. "Easy, Serena. I don't intend to castrate him."

"No cutting," Jack growled. "And I had him pretty contained."

"Yeah, whatever. Keon, is there a place to put him?"

"What? Like a dungeon? Before you guys came there wasn't anyone to put anywhere!" Keon chewed his lower lip, looking really worried.

"Stop it." Ice glared at them all impartially. "Okay. We'll set Tatiana on him or something. Jack, we need you working, not worrying about Tiny here."

"Hey!" Lane felt like he needed to object to that.

Shannon grumbled. "Damn it, I want to hurt someone. No one will let me."

"I'm not up for being kicked around, man."

"Nah, you're too little." Shannon sighed. "They wouldn't let me kick any ass when the Russians were here."

"Maybe you'll get a chance soon," Ice growled.

"I hope so."

"Well, no one is kicking this ass." Jack squeezed Lane's butt. "It's mine."

"Focus, you assholes!" The little guy, Gig, was hysterical.

Keon sighed, the sound long-suffering. "So, are we still mad at him?"

"Yes."

"No."

"What?"

"I'm going home." Lane was done with his. He was leaving, and Lane was taking baby Geri with him. She didn't need to live with these crazy people.

"Argh." Ice actually made the argh noise. "Okay. Jack, we need a strategy meeting. Now. If you have to bring him, bring him, but I want someplace that doesn't smell like spunk."

"I'm..." Lane was going to lose his shit.

"We'll be right there," Jack cut in.

"Good deal. You got five minutes."

As soon as they left, he burst out. "I didn't do it."

Jack grabbed his shoulders. "I know that, *cher*. If those big lugs would listen to their dragons, they'd know it, too."

Serena made an incredibly rude noise, the sound hilariously funny if you weren't afraid for your life.

Geri made a similar sound. A puff of smoke came out of her tiny nose.

"Oh, aren't you amazing?" Lane told her.

She preened for him, and everything seemed better. Brighter.

"Dragons don't lie," Jack said with a fond look at Serena.

"I don't either. I swear," Lane said. "That's what got me reassigned here. I tell if I fuck up."

"I believe you. Now, wash up and we'll go talk like reasonable men," Jack said with a smile.

"Reasonable. Right." Because a black ops team with mob mentality was reasonable.

"Oh, *cher*. We're actually capable of it. Prove you're an analyst and help us figure out who's trying to find us and why." Jack hugged him, a comforting press of flesh.

"Right. I mean, do they just want y'all home? Back to work? The bosses."

"I don't think so. I think everyone has found out about the dragons. Or think they have a clue about them. They don't really understand our babies." Jack grinned. "Okay, lady, I know you're not a wee one like Geri."

"No. No, she's a fine fierce lady." Lane believed that. Knew it.

Serena touched her muzzle to his shoulder. The dragons saw things so much more clearly than humans. Lane was learning them well already.

"So, you think they know about the dragons." Lane cleaned himself up, put his non-fucking brain on. "Everyone seems to know about the dragons."

"Not really. I think they're thinking in terms of a weapon. Something they can use. Like an attack dog. I seen what it takes for a dragon to attack, *cher*. It wears them plumb out."

"They're not dogs. I mean, I like dogs…" But he didn't want to use these guys for anything. They were complex, amazing creatures.

Geri trilled, rubbing her head on his arm, and he swore he saw an image in his head of her as a huge dragon, teeth bared as she protected him. "My bravest girl." She would be fierce. They were gonna have so much fun, and she would grow as big as Damien. "Wait. Who's Damien?"

Jack hooted. "Keon's dragon. She talking to you already?"

"Not in words, so much, but yeah, she's the one who gave me his name, I think."

"That's good, *cher*. Bond is already working hard for you."

"You ready for me to face the music?"

"I am." He felt as if Jack and Geri had his back. Maybe Serena.

"Let's go figure this shit out."

Jack stared Ice down as best he could with one eye. "I'm not tossing him out. No matter what Shan says. He's bonded with a dragon."

"Where did the beacon come from?" Ice asked Lane.

"I don't even know where y'all found it," Lane protested.

"Your go bag. Gig did a sweep."

Lane looked honestly surprised, which Jack had expected. "No. No way. I've dumped that damned thing out a dozen times looking for something."

"Where was it?" Jack demanded, his voice hard, choppy, even to his own ears.

"Between the bottom and the lining," Gig said, staring back and forth between them all.

"What?" Poor Lane, he kept saying that. Jack got it. He would be just as confused. Why send an analyst if your aim was spying on someone?

"So, if you didn't do it, who did?" Ice stared at Lane, arms crossed over his chest.

"I haven't seen anyone since the 'copter dropped me off. I flew in and they sent me on an ATV to find you. I just drove in the snow."

"Geri says he didn't do it," Keon put in, looking exhausted. Poor Keon, who'd had his life turned upside down. "Please. Please, I need life to be normal again. We all do. Stress is so bad for the dragons."

"Well, it's gonna be tough." When all of them glared at him, Jack shrugged. "The big bosses sent Ice. Then we came, then Lane. Not to mention the Russians. Someone has an agenda."

"Do I need to move the babies?" Keon was white as snow, panicked, looking ready to bolt.

"Not yet." Ice shook his head. "This is our most defensible position. We just have to make sure we account for everyone as much as possible."

"What can I do? I didn't mean to mess up," Lane murmured. Jack was so proud of his Lane for wanting to help people who were so suspicious of him.

Man, *his*. Already.

Fucking A.

"Okay." Shannon grunted and stroked his chin. "Do we destroy the beacon?"

"I've already spun it off two satellites." Gig looked up, wires in his mouth, fingers still typing. "I'm sending them to Australia first, then Peru."

"Good deal. I mean, they know our basic locale, but that will slow them down."

"We..." Lane chewed his bottom lip, brain obviously going ninety to nothing.

"We need to figure out what they want from us." Keon looked like he was gonna lose it. Ice was gonna be in so much trouble when he and Keon were alone.

"We could fake moving the dragons, maybe. Send fake communications," Lane said.

Gig actually looked at Lane with admiration. "Nice. I like that. Let them think we've abandoned the warren."

"Can we do that?" Jack wasn't sure if they could pull that off. Mountain was thermal, though, so maybe they could hide heat signatures.

Lane shrugged. "We can try. It can't hurt."

"True." Ice looked at Jack's boy with a new expression. "Nice one."

The radio crackled, and Chino, who was on watch, called in. "We got a problem, guys."

Jack closed his eye. Goddamn it. That was all they needed right now.

Ice grunted and grabbed the radio. "Go, Chino."

"There's an unmanned drone, boss. Heading directly for us. Surprised Gig didn't pick it up first."

"Shit." Ice studied each of them briefly, shaking his head at Keon. "No, it will be equipped with cameras. We can't let them see Damien."

Ah. Keon must have been suggesting taking it out with dragon power. Ice and Keon could talk to each other in their heads as easily as they could talk to the dragons.

"Shannon," Jack suggested. "Get the wind going."

"Sure. Sure, no problem." Shannon headed toward the door. "God, the air is still out there. Nothing to work with."

"You need something to start from, right?" Jack frowned. "Lane? Lane can help." Lane had that -- intensifier talent. Right?

"Yeah? I need a boost, man."

Lane shook his head. "I can't control what I do."

Jack stared at him. "You ever tried, *cher*?"

Lane shook his head, looking totally panicked.

"See? He's not gonna help. Fucking analyst." Gig was ramping up.

Jack saw Lane's eyes flash, felt a tingle slide up his arm and into Jack's fingertips. *Oui*. He knew it was in there.

"Shannon. Concentrate." Jack tugged Lane over to Shannon, then acted as their go-between, holding Lane's hand, then Shannon's arm.

He focused on Lane, on how much he wanted to touch, to play, to make the man scream. Lane blinked, and steam rose from Jack's skin where it touched Lane. Shannon jumped half a mile.

"Dude."

"Yeah, pretty fucking cool, huh?" Jack loved that his lover could boost them. Lane had a purpose beyond Geri, which was important to the Ops team.

Shan grinned wildly. "I get to kick some ass!"

"Uh-huh. Focus, man." Jack leaned down, whispered in Lane's ear. "I know you can do this, *cher*."

"I don't--" Lane paused, eyes wide. "The wind, Jack. I can feel it."

"Make it bigger, *cher*. Faster."

Lane frowned, and Jack could feel the energy surge through him. Shan cursed, but it was a happy noise.

"Fuck, yeah. You guys gotta feel this."

"No abusing my *choux*." Jack cackled, though, happy as hell with this new development.

The wind slammed through the bowl at the entrance to their cave, swirling up until it resembled a damned tornado. Jack could feel the pressure of it, the pull. Shannon was laughing as if he was some sort of evil genius in a movie, pushing harder at the wind with every breath.

Lane was damn near glowing, the man making everything swell and groan.

"Holy shit, Shannon!" Chino shouted over the radio. "Keep it up. You're about to blow that fucker out of the sky."

"More, Lane. I need more," Shannon said through gritted teeth.

"Trying."

Jack focused his energy, pouring steam into Lane. He could see it, Lane gathering the energy, growing it, pouring it into Shannon. Yes. He groped back with his other hand, and someone grabbed it, the freezing cold telling him it was Ice.

Lane arched, body jerking, the sudden rush of power making Shannon scream, the rush of wind turning into a gale.

"Shit! It's gone. The drone. Shattered. Jesus." Chino sounded awed, the radio signal breaking up some with the power of what had just happened.

Lane's knees buckled, a low cry filling the air.

"Lane!" Jack let go of Ice's hand so he could kneel next to his lover. "*Bebe*, you okay?"

"So big, *douce*. So big."

"Breathe. Geri is right here, *cher*. Let her help you."

"Geri?" Lane reached out for his wee one, the tiny dragon wrapping around Lane's throat after sliding up Lane's arm. They all laughed when Geri chittered at Lane as if scolding him.

"Good job, kiddo." Ice shook his head. "Chino? We're solid?"

"Yeah, boss."

"Okay. Hang out for another thirty, then Gig will spell you on watch."

"You got it. Chino out."

Jack glanced at Ice, then nodded to Shannon, who had plopped down on the floor, panting. "You guys will take care of Shan?"

"For sure." Ice grinned at him, looking less stressed by the second. "We're family."

"I know, *ami*." Jack tugged Lane to his feet, surprised that Serena had to move forward to hold him up. He'd given Lane a lot of steam.

Silly man. Her arch mental voice made him smile.

Your silly man. He loved her dearly already, so much that it made his chest hurt.

Sleep more? She nudged him with her snout. *Geri needs rest.*

We all do. Lane is already out like a light. Jack picked Lane up, in fact, and his lover smiled slightly.

"Hey," Ice said before he could leave. "Tell your man welcome to the team when he wakes up."

Serena chuckled, the sound echoing warmly in his brain. *It will be so crowded in here, Jack.*

Jack nodded and laughed, taking his lover and their dragons off for a nap. "It sure is, *ma fille.* I can't wait to see what happens next."

He had no doubt that it would involve heat. Heat and orgasms.

Vanished

Chapter One

Shannon rubbed his eyes, trying to ignore the pounding headache behind them.

Dragons. The whole bloody team had gone daft for the silly creatures. They were cute, he had to admit, and he did love the bright colors and amazing physical antics they produced.

What Shan didn't love was how he had a feeling the whole damned dragon operation was in danger now. Seemed too many people knew about the creatures, and their frozen mountain, and no one was able to think clearly enough with all the dragon bonding to figure out what to do. God knew, it was bad enough with the Russians and shit back at the beginning, but now they had analysts from their own government showing up, wanting to know why they weren't doing whatever job Ice had promised to do.

His head pounded like a kettledrum, boom-boom-boom, and Shannon swallowed back nausea. Maybe it was the altitude, but the last few days had just been brutal. He gulped big lungsful of the cold outside air and tried to get his head screwed on straight. Someone had to figure out what the fuck they were going to do.

"Hey." Gig slipped outside the mining office that served to hide the dragon compound. "You okay?"

Shan had a real fondness for Gig, who was their tech guy.

He didn't look much like a warrior, but all things electrical fell before him with his elemental talent. "Headache. Needed to get out of the inside for a bit."

"You want a migraine pill? I got some."

"Yeah, please." He would take them dry. "Where's your wee dragon?"

"Sleeping." Gig dug in one of a dozen pockets in his cargo pants before coming up with a bottle.

"He's a cutie." Cor was a tiny Asian dragon, and so shy. Shannon shook his head. "Weird, all this."

"Yeah. Yeah, I hear you. The whole thing reads like a set up."

"It does." Shannon hadn't really thought of it that way, but someone had to be pulling the strings for them to be getting so much flak. "We need to have a team meeting if we can pry everyone away from fucking or dragons."

"Well, I'm in. My dragon's sleeping and I can wait to jack off 'til we're done."

He blinked. Gig had never talked sex around him, even though Shannon would have welcomed the advances. "Uh, yeah. Maybe I ought to do that. Might help my headache."

"Possibly, yeah." Gig looked up into the sky. "Gonna snow again."

Shannon stifled a sigh. Yeah, he should know better than to think that was a come-on. No, it was just a friendly thing.

Of course, to make a liar of him, he could swear he felt a gentle touch to the small of his back, so quick he almost missed it. Shan breathed deep, Gig's scent strong on the air.

Shit. Should he say something? Hope Gig touched him again?

"You, uh… You doing okay?" he asked. They usually had a lot of downtime on missions, time to jaw with each other. Not this time, and he felt a little guilty for not checking in on Gig.

"Yeah. I'm good. How's your head?"

"Better," he lied. He had no idea why he had this perma-ache.

Gig's head tilted. "Is it like the worst headache ever?"

"I feel like I'm having a stroke, buddy." He rolled his head on his neck.

"Come with me?" Gig held out his hand.

"Where are we going?" Shan put his fingers in Gig's, let his buddy pull him inside.

"Trust me. I think I can help your head."

"I do trust you." He ached all over as if he had the flu.

"Good." Gig's thumb rubbed his palm. Okay, that was definitely touching on purpose.

That made a different part of his body ache.

Gig drew him deep into the mountain, into the sleeping chamber filled with dragons.

"What the hell, man?" All those beasts of all shapes and sizes... Shannon moaned, almost going to his knees when a fresh wave of pain hit him. "My head."

"Uh-huh. Which one?"

"Both." He grinned, a sad ghost of a smile, he was sure.

"Mmm. We'll talk about that later. I meant which dragon."

"What?" He had no idea what Gig meant. The dragons slumbered on, just snoozing, not one so much as twitching as far as Shannon could tell.

"Look. Which one makes it better?"

Shannon shook his head, stubbornly denying the possibility. He didn't have a dragon. Him and Chino, they were the only ones who hadn't bonded with one, right?

Chino, though, he wasn't having migraines.

"Trust me. Look. Come on."

Shannon blinked into the gloom, looking past the bright purple of Tatiana, the bright green of the one Keon called Norbert. They were larger, protecting the babies.

There was a little one -- she didn't even look real, but like something carved from amethyst -- and she was wide awake and staring at him.

Oh. Oh, God, she was beautiful. Her name was Estrella, which he knew suddenly, and she looked like a wee Mayan carving in purple.

Gig looked over and grinned, then walked over, picked the wee baby up, and eased her into Shannon's arms.

She chirped almost like a bird, and snuggled under his chin. Oh, fuck him. His head eased right off.

"Better?"

"Yeah. Wow. I mean. She's amazing." Was he wearing the same goofy face Gig had when he looked at Cor?

"She's beautiful." Gig kissed his forehead, lips warm and dry.

"She is. You're kissing me." He might explode if this day got any weirder.

"Just a little. Enjoy her."

"I don't mind. You want to meet us at the bathing room with Cor?" Somehow, he knew his girl wanted a bath. All the dragons seemed to love wallowing.

"I'd love that. I'll be there soon, huh? We'll soak."

"Sure." He hugged his little dragon girl close, listening to her song swell in his head.

She was soft, surprisingly warm. How could Jacques have denied this as long as he had? Shannon just hadn't known he had a dragon to bond with. Jack, man, he'd denied poor Serena deliberately, and for days. His skull had to be splitting still, he'd been so stubborn.

"You're like Cor, then, eh? Too darned young to really talk yet." He stroked her little brow ridge. She trilled for him, and he was hit right between the eyes with a wave of pure love. "My girl. My little star, eh? What a pretty baby." Okay, now he felt really sorry for Chino, the only one who hadn't bonded with a dragon.

She nuzzled his jaw, music filling his mind. Estrella. His Estrella. How had he missed her for days on end? "Are you shy, wee one?"

She was different -- none of the others were feathered, none of the others were so iridescent. Damn if she didn't suit him to the ground.

The others looked at him, and he thought there was approval

there. How sad, for some of the older dragons, to not know this bond yet, to not have access to humans to gain it.

He supposed they had Keon. God knew that man was obsessed with the critters. Now Ice, too, who could talk to all the dragons.

"Do you like Iceman, kiddo? He's always been so grumpy. Until now."

She chirped and clicked and his head was flooded with images of Ice and his dragon, Chi. The two were so happy, so in tune.

He chuckled. "Yeah. He's a sap." Curiosity hit him. Oh, she might not speak yet, but she could make herself clear. "A big softie, honey. A lover." He nuzzled his cheek against hers. His heart was totally full, so he guessed he was the same kind of softie.

She flapped and muttered, trying so hard to talk to him.

"I love you, too." He got it. She would get better as she got older, according to Keon. Her little feathery wings fluttered madly for him, the sound making him laugh. "Shall we go bathe?"

Oh, these little guys did love the water, didn't they? He got a distinct picture of how the hot water helped keep cold scales supple. Then snuggles and brushing with soft brushes.

"Oh, ho! Keon has you spoiled." He thought of all the rough field baths he'd had to take. This place had such a luxury pool, fed by hot springs.

Her nose wrinkled and he swore he could almost hear her distaste at the image of water out of a can like he'd used in the past.

"Better than sitting about stinking up the place."

She headbutted him, playing right back. Such a good girl. They were going to be the most amazing good friends. Shannon took Estrella down to the bathing cavern to find Gig and his Cor waiting.

If nothing else, he had to thank the man for getting rid of his headache.

Gig grinned, looking truly cheerful. "Better, huh?"

"God, yes."

"Excellent."

Cor was swimming happily, clucking and cooing at his girl. The two dragons splashed together as soon as Estrella abandoned Shan and splooshed into the pool.

"Thanks."

"I get it. I know about that ache."

"Yeah? So what about the other aches and pains? What do you do about those?"

Gig met his eyes. "Tug off a lot. Fantasize."

"About what?" Shannon figured he'd lost his mind coming on to Gig this way, but what the hell. He moved closer.

"You."

Well, he'd be damned. Shannon blinked, then chuckled. "You hid it well."

"You didn't seem interested."

"No?" He thought on that for a moment. "I guess after Ice and Spider went bad, I didn't want to mess with things."

"I can get that." A surprisingly callused hand touched his hip under the water.

"So, why now?" He thought he knew. Everything was changing, nothing as it was before.

"Everything's new, different. Life is a whole new game now."

"I guess so. Can I touch you?" He had a million other things he could say, but that popped out.

"God, yes." Gig checked the babies, who were chasing each other, gurgling and spitting happily. They were water safe, no doubt. They loved it.

Gig reached out, fingers sliding on his hip, his belly.

Shannon closed his eyes, letting his skin absorb the touch.

"You're fuzzy." That didn't sound like a complaint at all.

"Just so." Shannon knew he was a hairy ginger monkey. "You're all smooth."

"Mmmhmm. I bet there's some amazing friction there…"

Where had this delicious man come from? Shannon had never seen more than a glimpse of him before, but Gig was seducing him now.

It made no sense, but he wasn't complaining. No, he was gonna grab on and take what he could while he could.

Gig tugged his short hairs, pulling slow and easy, making it ache.

"Oh, damn." He pushed toward that hot hand, hips rocking.

"Mmhmm." Gig kept one eye on the dragons, one on him.

"Do we do this now, then?" He chuckled. "Maybe we should wait until they're asleep."

"Maybe. It's a little weird with the babies."

"Yeah." Lord love a duck. This had to be the first time he'd passed up sex for someone else's sake. Having a dragon was like having kids, he reckoned.

They grinned at each other, looking no doubt like the world's biggest fucking dorks.

"Let's swim, huh?"

"Works for me. I have a little one that needs chasing."

The babies splashed at them, cooing, and Shannon laughed out loud.

Gig moved through the water, sleek and more than a little amazing. The guy made Shannon feel a little like a big red ox -- fuzzy, lumbering, and slow.

"Cor!" Gig tugged a little tail, playing, teasing.

Cor made this great sound, obviously a laugh, and normally-somber Gig lit up.

He felt a tiny nibble at the end of his fingers, and glanced down to see Estrella gnawing on him. He hooted, flicking water at her with his other hand.

She spun around and slid up his back, bit his ear.

"Toothy beastie." He slid down in the water, which lost her purchase on his skin.

Her laugh tickled him, bone-deep. She had joy in her belly now that she'd found him, and she shared it with Shannon. Oh, his sweet girl.

He found himself a little dumbstruck, just staring. She flapped her wee wings, hovering on the water's surface. She made the barest waves in the water, fluttering about him. "Look at you. So light. Such a lovely lady."

"She's too cool," Gig said.

"She's fucking amazing."

Gig touched his butt as he floated by. "They're so neat. You get it now, huh? Why we have to keep them safe?"

"I got it before, man. I know it now in my soul, though."

These weren't animals. These were magic. Pure energy, a lot like him and his Ops boys. Only way less human, which was awesome. Not that Gig wasn't pretty awesome himself.

His girl draped herself over his arm, already tired out. "She's so little. Should we go nap?"

"Please." Gig smiled again, the look unfamiliar, warm, but so intriguing.

Shannon loved how it heated his whole body more than One-Eyed Jack's steam heat. Gig made him stupid. Had for a long time, but maybe now he could act on it.

"Come on, then." There would be time for the rest later. For now he had a dragon to bond with.

He'd done it.

He'd made a pass at Shan and the man had noticed. Finally. Wow. And also, woo.

Gig didn't dance or fist pump, but he did stare at Shan's hard, tight ass on the way back to their sleeping chamber, which was all comfy now, with blankets and pillows and lots of pads on the floor. Like a nest.

A dark, cozy nest, and they went all the way to the back to where the blankets were piled the highest, the deepest. Comfy at its best.

He and Shan settled together like spoons, with an ease that

belied them not touching before today. Cor made the happiest noise, sliding into the crook of his arm.

"Good boy. Just rest with me, hmm?" Cor nuzzled him, licked him a moment, which should have been so gross but wasn't. He chuckled softly, smoothing the delicate, tiny scales.

Little Estrella began snoring, and it made him and Shan both laugh.

"Somebody's tired." Of course, it was hard work, convincing a huge mass of a man to bond.

"She is." Shan chuckled. "I can't believe how deep she's sunk in me already."

"Keon says he's never seen it happen like this -- that there's something about us and our talents or whatever."

"Huh. Well, I ain't complaining." Shan shifted about, putting the babies together to let them snuggle off to one side. "Can we make out, now?"

"Mmmhmm." Gig lifted his blanket, making an offer that he hoped was clear.

Shan took the hint and slid close, big, hot body against his. It made his eyes cross a little bit, the contact, the heat. He'd waited so long. Then Shannon kissed him, and Gig moaned. He clung to Shan's shoulders, needing more. There was nothing quite like the pressure of Shan's body, rolling atop his.

The man was damned fine, and heavy, and hard as a rock for him.

Gig dragged one hand along the fat shaft of Shannon's cock, tracing the vein that throbbed there with one finger.

"Oh, fuck." Shannon rocked against him. "Are you real?"

"Digital."

"I bet, you weirdo." Shannon laughed, the Irish obvious in his voice.

That was him, weird, odd. Interesting. Gig grinned and reached down, cupped Shan's balls.

"Christ. That feels amazing."

"You are hung like a bull moose." He was impressed.

"Thanks." Shannon laughed again, the sound breathless. "Let me touch you, too."

That sounded like a fine idea. Better than any video game. Gig grabbed Shannon's ham-sized hand, placed it on his belly.

Shan stroked his skin, the heat of that touch amazing him, and he arched, his eyes going wide as he made an incoherent noise.

"Uh-huh. Yum." Shannon explored him, up to his chest, plucking at his nipples, then down below his waist. Gig's fingers were fascinated by Shan's fuzzy belly, and he had to tug at the hairs, had to comb through with his fingers.

"Not smooth like you."

"I like it." Gig tugged again.

"Good. I want you to want to do this again and again, okay?"

There wasn't going to be a problem with that. Gig had wanted this man for so long, had watched and waited for his chance.

He'd tried to make offers, but no one had noticed. Not even a little. They'd all been so different just a few short weeks ago. The dragons had opened them all to new possibilities, made them braver.

He leaned forward, kissed the curve of Shan's jaw. The tiniest movement had their mouths meeting in a kiss, Shannon taking control easily.

Gig pushed up and over, straddling Shan's waist.

"Horny bugger." Shannon grabbed his ass and squeezed.

"Is that bad?" Sex was good cardio, right? He needed to keep his stamina up.

"No. No, it's the best." Shan arched up, almost unseating him.

Oh, this was a little like riding a mechanical bull. That and tequila could make a good night. Shan was gonna be better than good. Shannon was going to turn him inside out.

"You want to ride, huh? I can do that. Gotta get a kit bag, though."

"Mmhmm. I like riding." He kept his voice pitched low.

"Good. Oh, honey, we're gonna have so much fun together."

Was this real? Could it be real after so long? He didn't dwell on it, bending instead to kiss Shan again, the flavor of that hot mouth addictive.

His cock was full, the ache in his balls familiar, while the promise of touch was new. Shannon stroked his lower back, his butt, making the happy noises.

It was amazing, the way Shan's hands traced his body, touched him as if he was fascinating. He felt a tiny draft swirl through the room, the wind power gaining ground. His electricity fought to respond and he yanked the temptation back. No. No shocks. Not if he wanted Shannon having fun instead of pain.

Shannon laughed when the static sparked between them. "Crackling."

"Yes. Sorry. I try to keep it together."

Shannon snorted. "Totally overrated."

Shan drew him down into another hard, toothy kiss. God, that rocked his world. His dick was aching, he was so hard.

Gig rubbed along the soft, fuzzy belly, his cockhead dragging and leaving slick trails.

"Sweet. Love how you feel."

All Gig could do was moan, push the sound into Shan's lips. He held on, hips rocking. Shan's hand was on his ass, pushing him, driving them together. More friction. Christ. "Gonna," he warned, knowing there was no way he'd last through fucking. "Close."

"Good." Shannon grunted the word out, his face drawn in a grimace.

He nodded and bit at Shan's collarbone, balls tightening as he shot.

"Fuck! Gig. Oh, God." Shannon came for him, that big, magnificent body bucking under him.

Oh, hell yes. He nodded and kept moving, let the pleasure go on and on. The last spasm finally faded, and he flopped down, patting Shannon's wide chest.

"Mmm. That was so much better than whacking off."

"No shit on that," Gig concurred. Very much. His head bobbed, and he was so tired suddenly, kind of like the baby dragons in their care.

"C'mere." Shannon drew him down, cradled him, arms around him. So warm.

He snuggled right in, wiggling until they found where they fit together. He loved the way Shannon felt like a big, live mattress.

Shannon stroked his hair. "Shh. Sleep."

"Trying." He yawned, and Cor murmured, then came to crawl up on his shoulder. Estrella came to Shannon, and suddenly Gig couldn't keep his eyes open.

Boom.

Chapter Two

Shannon grinned at the ceiling. He couldn't believe he and Gig had, well, done the deed. Explosively. Happily. Naked. Woo.

Estrella grumbled, her tail wrapping more tightly around his arm. She slept deep and hard, and his thoughts were waking her. Her little *grrr* made him laugh.

She rattled her scales at him, clicking and clacking for his benefit. Her tiny feathers ruffled right up, and he stroked them back down. "You are the most lovely of all dragons. So beautiful and amethyst."

Her entire tiny body blushed, she was so pleased with his praise.

"I see you've learned to talk to a dragon the only way they'll accept."

Shannon jumped half a foot when Keon's voice broke the silence. Christ, the dragonkeeper was quiet. And in his personal space. "Did you need something?"

"Ice and Jack say we need to have a meeting. Sorry. I know you guys are tired."

"No problem. Give us ten or so."

"Meet us in the kitchen? I've made soup."

Shannon grinned, thinking how Keon coddled all of them. "Thanks, Mom."

"Shut up." Keon chuckled, chucked Estrella under the chin. "Lucky girl."

"He's the lucky one," Gig said from his perch on Shannon's chest.

"You get it, don't you?" Keon beamed, looking so proud to share his friends, his dragons.

"Of course I do." Gig thumped Shannon's chest.

"Hey, I'm learning." Slow but sure, that was his way. Well, unless it involved the wind.

Estrella whistled, making a sound like a breeze.

"That's right, baby girl. Windy me."

She chortled and flapped and he loved on her, telling her how he loved her.

Gig dressed, whistling happily. Happy. Gig. Wow. His little poster child for depression was suddenly all smiles. Shan tugged on sweats.

He barely felt the brush of Gig's fingers on his ass.

Shannon jumped, then blinked. Forward man. That was surprising. Stunning. He didn't expect Gig to be so sexual. Thank God he was. Sexual and interested.

He planned to explore that a lot more. For now he'd let Keon feed them. Gig let Cor drape over his shoulders, the wee dragon looking perfectly happy.

"Hey, man, look at you, all dragon-ed." Ice clapped him on the shoulder when he walked into the kitchen room.

"She's beautiful, isn't she?" Shannon was so proud he couldn't bear it. Estrella made him feel tall as the mountain they were on.

"Stunning. Such a color. And feathers." Ice chucked Estrella under her chin.

"He is a good man, sweet girl." Keon grinned. "Made for you."

She made this amazing noise, one of complete agreement, and love for her almost choked him it got so big. Such trust. How did it happen so fast?

"They're way smarter than we are," Keon said. "They know."

Estrella jangled and fluttered for him. He loved how hard she was trying to talk to him. "Soon, wee girl. Soon. I know it."

"She will. She's so young." Keon looked so fond. "She's eager to learn, though. She'll talk before Cor, I bet."

Cor made a disgusted noise and shook his wee head, so righteous. The cute almost overwhelmed Shannon.

"You don't think so, brilliant boy?" Gig was too damned adorable, too. Shannon knew the happiness bubble was about to burst with this meeting, but damn he felt good.

Keon's face lifted, like he was listening to someone, a fond smile on his lips.

Ice blinked, then chuckled. "Damien wants to remind you that all of these guys will get bigger than we puny humans."

"Puny?" Shan puffed up. He was not on the small side, damn it. Nothing puny about him.

Keon laughed. "Tatiana is bigger than us and she's a youngling still."

"They're all perfect. All of them."

Chino strode into the room, stripping off cold weather gear. "Yep. Perfect." He snorted. "You vatos are losing it."

"Fuck off, man. How's the snow?"

"Not deep enough." Chino sighed. "I think we got more movement down the hill."

Gig groaned and pulled up his laptop, then started typing, slender fingers moving in a blur. The surveillance cameras began scrolling across his screen, pictures popping up.

"There's another cell of soldiers. Not sure whose. We've got to get them to back off." Gig looked willing to destroy them all, his face set in angry lines.

Shannon understood that now. Not that he didn't always love a good battle, but how were they going to keep them from just coming and coming in waves?

"Damien wants to go bathe. Do you guys need me for this?" Keon had dished up food and was now cleaning countertops.

"Are you useful?" Jacques asked.

"Not even a little."

They all chuckled, but Ice pulled Keon over for a quick, hard kiss. "I can keep you posted through Damien. Go on."

Keon rubbed noses with Ice and headed off, Ice's eyes never

leaving the man's body. That was hot as hell. Shannon got that now, too, because he could hardly look at Gig without getting hard. Crazy, how this mountain had changed them all. Well, except Chino.

"What are we going to do, boss?" Gig asked. "We can't leave them unprotected."

"Well, I'm not leaving." Ice shrugged. "Still, we can't move them either. Nowhere else will we find a set up like this. So, somehow we have to make them vanish."

Lane, the government analyst who'd ended up all tangled with Jacques, raised a brow, looking dubious. "How do we do that?"

"What if we move the entrance? Make it to where they think we've left?" Gig was a brilliant son of a bitch.

"Misdirection." Jack nodded before slurping up his stew. "I like it."

"We block up the entrance, camouflage it, make a new one. Bang. We can make it look good, as though we're gone."

Chino blinked. "What are we, the Army Corps of Engineers? How are we supposed to make a new entrance in a mountain?"

"I bet the big guy can do it." That big dragon had to have another out, right? Damien wouldn't fit through the door they used.

"Shit, yeah," Ice said. "Damien can melt rock, and with Lane to help direct the power…" Lane had the power to enhance any of their talents with a single touch--

Before they could even open their mouths again, dragons all jumped to their feet, bodies stiff, teeth bared, and then, about a second later, he heard a wild scream, a sound of pure horror.

Ice fell to his knees, hands clutching his head.

"What the fuck?" Gig stood up, laptop sliding off his lap. "Ice? Cor? What's going on?"

It was Jack who grabbed his gun from the rack by the door and started running. "They've got them!"

Chino went next, with Shannon and Lane following. Ice was

out of commission, but Gig would stay with him and man the main compound.

Protect the little ones.

God, someone had to protect them.

Serena roared out her fury, the sound wild. The larger dragons began to appear on the slope as they ran, a flurry of wings and scales.

"Come on, Ice. Keep it together. Chi? Come here and hold him," he heard Gig shouting as they left the compound.

Jack seemed to know where they were going, thank God. Shan would have headed for the big bathing chamber, but Jack led them outside, pelting down a path Shan had never seen. Serena took off, her wings beating like a giant drum.

Her screams were wild, furious, fire belching from her, even harder and hotter than their old fire elemental, Damon, could create it.

Damn, if that was what Estrella would be someday, he was gonna love this shit. Right now, though, he needed to concentrate on the situation.

"Jack! Check in." Shit, they needed their headsets. Jack was too far ahead. Jack was just running blind, storming ahead, making so much noise, warning anyone they might be coming. All of their fucking training was out the window. Man, you bonded psychically with a dragon and all your military smarts disappeared.

"Damien is down," Jacques screamed. "They have Keon."

"Have him how?" What the fucking fuck? How could anyone have slipped up on them this badly? They'd really been basking in the glow of new bonds, for sure. He rounded a bend in the trail, a steaming body of water three times the size of the bathing room hanging on the side of the mountain. Holy shit, look at that.

Damien was there, skin almost a pale pink, blood dripping from his mouth. The track of the soldier cell was long and wide. No one was trying to hide this or the trail of blood spatter heading down the mountainside.

Jesus.

Shan had no idea what to do for a dragon, but he was a medic, damn it. He slid to a stop, hand on Damien's long neck. "Hey, buddy. Look at me, huh?"

He swore he could hear a deep pounding, like the beat of a huge heart. The sound repeated, "Keon, Keon, Keon," over and over.

"Okay, Damien. Okay, we'll get him back." Shannon checked to see where the blood came from. "Can you show me where you hurt?"

Damien moaned, the sound like fault lines shifting.

"Come on, now. Let me help. We can do this."

Damien tilted that massive head, letting him see the slash under his vulnerable jaw.

"Jesus fucking Christ." He grabbed Chino, tore the flak jacket off the man and pressed it to the wound. No. No way. No fucking way was this happening.

Chino growled, the sound feral. "Goddamn it. I need to provision. Jack is tracking them. I'm getting our gear. You take care of the big guy."

"You get Ice up and fucking moving and get me access to comms." Shannon needed eyes and ears on the situation.

"You got it." Chino sprinted off, leaving him with an injured dragon and a half frozen body. His own.

"I should have put on more clothes, huh?" Shannon jabbered away, making sure the sparkling eye stayed fastened on him. Damien wasn't in danger of bleeding out, but damn, that was nasty. Someone had cut him good.

"We're going to get Keon back, and we're going to fix this. I swear."

A dragon about the size of a Saint Bernard appeared next to Shannon, a go bag clutched in its mouth. Chino couldn't have gotten shit together that quick, so Gig was thinking on his feet.

"Good baby. Oh, thank you." Shan heaped praise on the

dragon, knowing this had to be terrifying.

The little one bowed for him, then went to nuzzle Damien. Yeah, comfort was good, and this one could help stand guard.

"You see anything that's not me or one of mine, kiddo, you holler. Got it?"

The dragon's head bobbed, and then another three colorful creatures came with more supplies, a radio, and sharp eyes.

Damn, that was handy. He sent a wave of comforting thoughts to poor Estrella, back at HQ with Gig. She was too small for combat. Then he slipped on his headset. "Sitrep, Gig."

"They're heading East, Shan. They're dragging Keon. He's naked. He's gonna freeze, man."

"Damn it. Jack should be close by now." Serena would fry the bastards. Right? "What's Ice's condition and where the hell is Lane?"

"Ice is coming to. He's almost forming words. I haven't seen Lane..."

Chino came on the comm. "Lane bugged out with Jacques. He's fast for an analyst. Hopefully he can help Steam and his orange girl get those bastards. I'm on my way back to you, Shan."

"Ten-four."

"Give me that." He heard a rustle and a little feedback, then Ice sounded. "What the fuck is going on?"

"They took Keon. Jack, Lane and Serena are on their backtrail. I have Damien secure, but he's injured. I have plenty of dragon backup."

"Who is they, Shan?"

"Fuck if I know. Ask Damien, man." He hadn't seen the perps, had no idea who they were.

"He's... confused. He's saying it was us, and we were all here."

"Then they weren't Russians." Chino sounded grim. "Damn it to fucking hell and back. Our own people are doing this to us!"

"Who the hell knows who they were? We've got to get him back." Ice sounded fucking panicked.

"We intend to. Get yourself together, damn it." He was tired of this shit. They were going to get Keon, leave a fucking messenger out of these assholes to send the note that dragons were not on the menu, and then move the entrance to the caves.

Period.

Well, then he was going to fuck Gig into the floor. Twice.

Then period.

Shannon actually allowed himself to grin. Damien's blood was coagulating well now, so he wrapped the survival blanket around the wide neck to keep the makeshift bandages in place before yanking on his clothes, the cold almost mitigated by the steam from the hot springs.

Keon. The single word was filled with pain, loss, and it was the biggest damn sound he'd ever heard.

"No!" Ice screamed it. "He's okay. I'm going to find him, Damien."

The dragon's huge head landed on the ground with a thump that rocked Shannon. "Ice? Ice, boss? What the fucking fuck?"

"Keon is out cold. Damien can't reach his mind and thinks they killed him. Drugs, I bet." He could hear Ice moving on the headset now. "I'm coming."

"Good. He's not dead."

"Nope. Just out. I would know." Ice grunted. "Hell, for me it's easier. Quieter in my head."

Chino chugged up to Shannon just then, tossing more supplies at him. "Leave the big guy with his baby guards. We're going after the dragon whisperer."

"Okay. You're sure?" Shannon didn't know a lot about dragon physiology, but Damien wasn't looking so good.

"Yeah. What he needs is his man." Chino sounded so sure, and Shannon was damned worried about the rest of his team. When Tatiana settled in beside Damien and flapped her wings at him, Shannon nodded.

"We're Oscar-Mike, Gig. On the move," Shannon said.

"They're heading down again, moving slower, but leaving

hella tracks. I'm going to buzz them with our little drone." Gig was ready to kick ass; it came across clearly in his voice.

"Good deal." Shannon and Chino could move fast now that they were both clothed against the weather.

"I'm heading down through the mountain itself. Keon says there's a hidden exit here. Maybe I can cut them off."

"Good deal. Keep in touch as much as you can."

Now they just needed to figure out how to get ahold of Jack, who was still off the comm loop.

"Hey, Iceman. Can you get Serena to tell Jack we need him?"

"On it." Ice went silent for several moments. "Gig, get one of the fast fliers to take Jack a headset. He's maybe a thousand yards from the perps but he needs backup."

"Yes, sir. Bella? Baby? Can you help me?"

He heard a hard chirp, and knew a dragon would be winging to Jacques in no time. "Tell her to stay low, Gig. Not be a target." Shannon worried, damn it. Bella was so young.

"Stay low, baby. Hide, hide, hide. Go to Jack and be safe."

Shannon saw Bella go overhead maybe a minute and a half later, a shadow moving so fast she could have been a large bird. God, he loved these magical creatures. Loved them. He hoped he had the kind of long life Keon said they could exploring his bond with his girl.

They slowed down, the sounds of voices floating up on the wind.

"Okay. We need to coordinate."

"I vote for razing them all. Fuckers," Gig said.

"Leave one alive," Ice murmured.

Chino nodded. "Just one, boss."

Shannon shared a glance with Chino just as Jacques came online, his Cajun accent right there. "They stopped. Some kind of malfunction of their equipment."

"You got eyes on Keon?" Ice sounded deadly calm.

"Yessir." Jack was out of breath, but otherwise understandable. "He's out cold."

"Cold is the operative word," Lane added in.

"Yeah, no shit. He's naked and blue."

"I've got provisions for him." Ice was going to kill everything in sight, Shannon could tell.

"We need to take them, boss. We can't keep playing this game." Gig sounded furious.

"No. No, we can't. Okay, Jack, you and your man Lane get around on their retreat side if they've stopped. Keep that big orange girl quiet for a few more minutes. Shan, you and Chino try to cut off the other angles that are not the direct path back here. I've got that one." Ice was back to fighting form, and it gave Shannon confidence.

"You got it, boss." Protect the primary, keep one alive.

"Focus on the job," Jack agreed. "And rev your engines. We'll need all our abilities."

Ah, the call of the elemental ops team.

Suddenly he wished Gig was there with him physically, not just on the radio.

Gig's voice crackled over the com. "I got your back, Shan."

His eyebrow went up, the words surprising him. Chino chuckled next to him, and Shannon glared at him.

"What? Everyone's fucking falling in love," Chino said, waggling his brows.

"You feel like the odd man out?" Man, was Chino gonna leave once they were safe? That would suck.

"Not a bit. I'm a loner; you know me."

"I do." Chino could do surveillance for weeks on his own, only reporting in when he had to. "You want the right flank?"

"Works for me. Let's go create mass chaos."

"Fuck, yeah." Shannon took the left, splitting away from Chino, letting the windstorm build up in his chest.

Time to play.

Chapter Three

Gig watched the attack from the drone's camera, focused on the movements of the kidnappers, warning the team of trouble.

"Shan, to the left."

"Ice! Incoming!"

He felt removed, like he was just a sportscaster, calling plays after the fact. Those were his guys down there. His lover. God, he was worthless up here.

"Chino, keep above them." Gig was trying to help, though.

Damien was beginning to wake up, move around, Gig's electronic eyes on the ground staticky from the proximity to the huge dragon, but still functional. Gig wanted him in the fight, and was trying to figure out how to get him up and pissed off.

The little ones guarding Damien were pushing and nosing the big guy, trying to get him up moving. Good. Good babies. Gig keyed up the closest camera to Damien and sent a gentle nudge of electricity through the line.

Wake up, you. Keon needs you.

Damien lifted his head, blinking.

Whoa.

Whoa, had Damien heard him? Maybe he had a special emergency direct line.

I'm serious. He sent a jolt of energy. *Keon needs you.*

My Keon. Damien roared, rising to a crouch, his wings spreading, his color deepening to a darker red.

He'd be goddamned. "Yeah. Yeah, man. That's it."

The sight of Damien taking off into the sky was like nothing else Gig had ever experienced. Awesome in its power. Terrifying.

"He's coming, guys. Damien. He's coming. Now."

Ice grunted, caught in a hand-to-hand struggle. "Follow my voice, big guy."

Keon! The roar split the air, threatened to crack his head wide open like a melon. Gig reeled, his ears ringing, and Cor climbed into his lap, tiny paws patting his cheeks.

"Oh, God." That hurt. So bad.

A chittering sound was his answer, Cor rubbing cheeks with him before turning his head toward the screen. He swore he could feel Cor cheering Damien on.

God knew, Gig was doing the same.

"Shan! Behind you!" His heart leaped into his throat when a soldier took Shannon down from behind, but Shan blew the man right off. Literally, with a gust of wind. Okay, that was still the hottest thing ever, watching Shan use his elemental power.

Still, after getting to touch and taste.

Gig grinned, feeling every pulse of his team's talents when they used them.

Somehow this situation had turned from horror to anticipation. Was that fucked up? He wanted to kick some ass. Wanted the whole world to know their dragons were off limits. That the team were off fucking limits.

Ice sent a slice of frozen air at one soldier, who stumbled back.

He buzzed the drone straight through the center of the troops, making them scramble. He wanted eyes on Keon.

Poor guy. No one had gotten to him yet, and Ice was going nuts.

He kept the drone low, hoping it would cause enough confusion to keep them off Keon, at least. Then he sent a little crackle of electricity through it, not enough to burn it out, but enough to startle.

The wind picked up visibly, and lightning crashed, Chino getting in on the game.

Keon's eyes opened, and Gig could tell, even through the drone's camera, that they weren't human anymore. Not a bit.

Shannon felt the surge of power that swept the clearing the moment Keon woke up. He knew it was Keon, because all of the dragons roared, including Damien, and Christ, his ears wouldn't stop ringing.

The group of soldiers had stopped because they were waiting for backup, their GPS down, and the tide had turned against Shan and his guys when the second cadre had shown up.

He had a feeling it was about to swing the other way.

A surge of flame poured from Keon, incinerating all the soldiers around him, turning them into ash. Shit, he hoped that Keon knew friend from foe and didn't burn any of the elemental ops guys down.

Lane shouted, the little Cajun sounding like a banshee with his rebel yell, and a flash of steam cooked another set of the enemy like a Christmas pudding. Christ, that was a hell of a talent, being able to intensify their skills.

Damien landed behind Keon, surprisingly delicate for such a huge motherfucker. Damien wrapped around his guardian and began to wreak havoc.

The place turned into a volcano. Ice stepped up to protect his team with well-placed ice floes, which was probably the only thing keeping their skin from blistering.

Damien took to the air, carrying Keon with him, setting a huge section of the forest alight with a single gusty breath.

Chino screamed, the sound one of a hunting warrior. Shannon whipped up a gust of wind to drive the flames, push whoever might be interested back down the mountain.

Jacques was shouting something in his French patois, but Shannon got the message. Time to regroup and present a hard line instead of fighting individually.

Gig's drone was following the retreating troops, moving fast. Good man. Lane was standing next to Chino now, and little crackles of lightning chased the men, too.

Together, they created pure chaos, and the snow began to fall, heavy and wet, with ice pellets beating down.

The last of their opponents fell, about fifteen of them having made a run for it, only about five having stayed to fight.

Some men were just born fools. These guys died just like idiots, too.

Bella came flying back to them, landing near Ice and making these amazing noises. Her report on the fleeing soldiers, no doubt.

As far as he was concerned, it was time to go the fuck home.

"Report," Gig said over the comm. "Roll call."

"Here. Is Keon there with you yet?" Ice snarled the words out.

"Haven't seen them."

"Jack, aye."

"I'm here," Lane said, so not military.

"Chino in."

"Good deal. Are you ready to retreat yet?"

"Yep." Shannon glanced at Ice. "Can you contact his dragon, man?"

"Damien's not talking to me. He's… he's pissed off."

"Oh." Well, that sucked. At least he could hear Gig on the comm. Speaking of…"How's my dragon, Gig?"

"She's snuggling with Cor. We're being brave." He could hear Gig grin.

"Good for her. I'm proud."

Jack gave him a look, a wink. "Loser."

"What? Me?" He laughed. "Nah. That's Chino."

"Shut up, fuckmonkey." Chino threw a snowball at him.

Lane's teeth chattered. "Can we go back inside now?"

"They'll have to back off long enough for Ice to convince Damien to seal the door, right?"

"They will." Gig's voice came loud and clear. "They're not gonna regroup on the mountain. The drone shows full retreat."

Ice nodded. "No way can they get us with the snows coming. There's a hell of a storm brewing."

"Imagine that," Jacques drawled. "Make tracks. Serena says Keon is in the bathing room thawing out."

"Let's go. Come on. Hurry." Ice looked near desperate, and it wasn't a good thing.

"We're coming. You make tracks." They would follow him up, clean up the back trail.

"Thanks. Gig, watch their asses."

"No problem, boss!"

Shannon humped his ass back up the trail, needing to see Gig, to see his baby girl Estrella. Touch them.

Know that they were safe -- his family.

God, how fucked up was this? He'd gone from hard-bitten soldier to weird-ass family man in no time. Like without even actually fucking Gig yet.

Oh.

Fucking. Gig. This was a fabulous idea. Naked. Sliding into tight heat and ramming until he came. Shan did love to get busy after battle. And this had been a wickedly good battle.

Shannon grinned, adding a little kick to his pace. He needed. Now.

Now, worked for him. The cold couldn't touch the heat building inside him.

Gig spoke in his earphone, echoing his thoughts. "Come home."

"I'm coming, baby." He didn't care who heard him. Ice had left them in a trail of snowy air, trying to get to Keon, and Jack and Lane were crazy for each other, already touching.

Chino was a psycho and a half. Shan had no idea what kind of creature it would take to keep up with that longtime loner. He hoped Chino found out someday, but right now that was the least of Shannon's worries.

"Good." Gig's single word said a lot.

Like a lot a lot, the tone hot as Damien's fire. Damn. His whole body tightened, ready to go. Revved up. Woo.

The trek back seemed to take forever and, by the time they slipped inside, the snows were fierce. You couldn't mess with shit as much as his team did and not have a backlash from Mother Nature.

Estrella met him right inside, her tiny purple body shaking, her little voice scolding him. Oh, poor wee love. "Sorry, baby girl. You did so good, taking care of Gig and Cor." He shucked his coat and opened his arms, tugging her close. She felt as cold as he did, and he realized how connected they were just then.

He carried her, heading for Gig, Cor, all of them. His fucking family.

Gig came to him, arms open. "Everyone is back, and the alarms are set on the cameras. Chino assures me he has the comm."

"Good deal. Come on." They needed to connect, to touch and feel that they were all fine. Shannon needed Gig's warmth.

Then, once they were alone, he needed Gig's tight little ass.

He grinned, sliding an arm around Gig's waist, and that earned him another of those rare smiles. Shannon could get addicted to those. It was like they'd appeared for him and only him.

Shannon took Gig to their little sleeping nest. Cuddling with dragons first. They needed him like no one ever had. That was something he'd never expected to have.

Gig left Shannon and the little ones snoozing and then headed to check on Keon. That whole naked in a blizzard and having crazy dragon eyes in your head thing couldn't be healthy.

Shan was the medic, but hey, he'd had a rough day, too. Gig had been safe and warm the whole time. Not only that, Gig had the sneaking suspicion that what was wrong with Keon, Shan couldn't fix.

They did field triage, not major dragonkeeper maintenance.

He peeked around the corner, not wanting Damien to fry his ass, thinking he was an enemy. "Just me, guys? Boss? You there?"

"Yeah. We're in here," Ice said.

"Keon okay? You guys need anything?"

"I don't know." Ice still sounded a lot freaked out.

Gig headed in, Damien lifting that huge head to stare at him. "Hey, man. You know me, huh? I know you do." They had a wee bit of a connection. Just a tiny one. He'd been the one to get Damien up and moving, right?

Damien nodded gently, blinking slowly.

Oh, yeah. Better. There. Okay. Keon was asleep, it looked like, but he was too pale, too still. "Can I help?"

Ice's little blue dragon was draped over his shoulders, obviously trying to give comfort, because Ice's expression was devastated.

Gig took about ten seconds to review the situation. Then he set his jaw and nodded. Okay, they had fought the soldiers as a team, they would do this together, too. "I'll be right back, Iceman. You hang in there."

Right. Team. Dragons. All the good things. A plan. Woo. Together they should be able to help Keon, damn it. Gig ran, going for Shannon first.

"Shan! Get up."

"Wha' s up, man?" Shan reached for him and the temptation to just cuddle in was huge.

Keon needed them, though, and the man had opened his home to them, given them the gift of dragons. Time for them to give back, help the poor dude wake up. "Keon needs us."

"Okay, let's go. Us as in you and me us or us all the team?"

"Us all of us."

"I'll find Chino. You get Jack and his new boytoy."

Gig chuckled, but nodded, heading off to find their Cajun, the others. "Keon needs us, guys!"

Jack came out of the bathing room, wet as a mad dog. "Us?"

"The team and our dragons. Bring Lane."

"You got it." Jacques was solid, nodding and turning tail to get his man.

That was the best, knowing he could call and his team would answer, no matter what.

Shannon appeared with Chino, the little purple dragon riding Shan's arm.

Sweet girl. He rubbed her under the chin, tickling her. "Hey, pretty girl."

Estrella wiggled, but she looked sad, really. He'd bet all the dragons were out of sorts.

"Let's go help Damien, hmm? Help them both?"

Estrella snorted and Cor came to Gig, ready to jump on the bandwagon. Serena came, with Lane and his wee one, too.

And there they went, a parade of soldiers and dragons and one weird little analyst.

Hoo-boy.

Gig had always felt as though his team was his family, but he'd never felt a part of something this big, like he could make a difference in something real.

They all went to the big room behind the curtain, where Damien and Keon slept, and where Ice had moved in with his Chi. Damien was cuddling close to Keon, breathing slow.

Poor guys.

"Okay, Ice, help us out. We need to get close."

Tatiana dared to reach for Damien, one clawed paw on his neck.

Damien sighed, the sound one of relief, and he knew he was on the right track. "Ice, you touch Keon."

"No problem, man. None." Ice gathered Keon close.

"Okay, Lane? Do you mind being our go-between? You put your hands on Ice."

Lane chewed his lower lip, pondering, before nodding. "Might work."

"It'll work." He knew it. Damn it. Gig believed.

"Okay." Lane put his hands on Ice's shoulders, and the rest of the team circled Lane, touching their own personal amplifier.

He held Cor and he held Shan's hand. "Okay, guys. Think happy thoughts. Whole, healthy good things so we can all play in the water together."

Ice chuckled, the sound like sandpaper over rock. "Yeah. Come on, guys."

Dragons came in droves, filling the space with heat and bodies, large and small. Power hummed through the room, raising the hair on Gig's arms and on the back of his neck.

Shannon looked down at him, then just bent and took his lips in a hard kiss. Boom.

Right there. An eddy of wind swirled in the room, a tiny little crackle of electricity running along the walls.

"Come on, Keon. Come back to us." Ice's whisper was heartbreaking.

Damien made a sound, half groan, half laugh, and Gig was amazed at how clear the big guy was in his communication. The other dragons moved closer, wings and tails twining together.

The colors of the dragons were growing brighter, clearer by the second. Damien seemed to grow, his skin filling in with health, the wrinkles disappearing.

Oh, hell yes.

It was working. It was. Thank God. Keon's skin lost its icy pallor, beginning to turn pink with the warmth they generated.

Ice laughed suddenly. "Oh. Oh, babe. There you are. I can hear you."

Keon frowned, his lips moving. Score. Come on!

Damien stretched, scales slithering and sliding over stone and blankets. The movement looked fluid, graceful. The whole room shifted, all the bodies inside reacting to Damien's.

One by one the wee dragons began to move, to shiver and

shake and make noise and Gig knew that they were calling to their Guardian.

Their Keon.

Keon twisted in Ice's grip, arching a little, pressing against Damien. Damien made a happy sound, his huge snout rubbing Keon's crazy black hair.

A warm wave seemed to come from Damien and they all relaxed as a single unit.

"Why are you all in my room?" Keon asked, sounding so confused.

Ice laughed, squeezed Keon tight. "Helping, babe. They were helping."

"Oh. Hi." Keon blinked, eyes finally opening, and a happy sigh went through the crowd.

Shannon squeezed his fingers, hard, and he squeezed back. They'd done it. They'd healed Keon.

Jacques whooped, a drawn-out Cajun sound, and Chino ululated.

The tension left Gig in a rush, leaving him weak-kneed, boneless. Shannon caught him, hugging him tight, taking another kiss that made his head spin.

Oh.

He pushed into the kisses, forgetting for a second that they had an audience. A rather considerable one, both human and dragon.

"The dragons say go get a room. All of you." Ice chuckled a little. "Go on. Oh, and thank you. They'll stay in here with us tonight. Keon and Damien could use the connection."

"Yeah?" Shannon looked all, uh, feral all of a sudden. Hot as hell.

Ice nodded. "Shoo. Let us get settled."

"Good deal." Shannon grabbed his hand and began to tug him out of the room. They were almost at the door when he heard Keon.

"Thank you, Gig. You're kind of amazing."

He grinned, feeling like he'd really done the best he could to help the team up close and personal. "You're welcome."

Chapter Four

Shannon wanted Gig right now. Right now. He had waited long enough. Damn it. He looked at the others. "The big sleeping area is ours. You go to the bath."

Jack and Lane chuckled, but disappeared like smoke. Chino just snorted. "I'll keep watch again, huh? Someone spell me in a bit so I can sleep."

"Thanks." He didn't even have time to feel sorry for Chino. That ass was calling his name, tight and tiny and attached to Gig. They had time alone, and he wasn't gonna waste it.

He pounced as soon as they got into the room, jumping on his lover and driving Gig down to the cushions.

Gig grunted, but wrapped around him, arms and legs clinging to him.

Yeah.

Fuck, yeah.

He took the kiss he wanted to -- all teeth and pressure, taking no prisoners. He lifted Gig with one hand under that little bubble butt, rubbing hard. The feel of it made him fucking dizzy, made him growl.

Gig wiggled. Fucking wiggled and rubbed and bounced.

"When did you get energetic?"

"Hey! I worked hard today." Gig grinned hugely.

Gig had been amazing, even. Clever. Now Shannon wanted Gig incoherent. So he started touching, squeezing those butt cheeks while he bit at Gig's neck. Oh, nummy. Hot spot.

He fastened on, sucking up a mark and listening to Gig

moan. Shan loved how that made Gig arch and beg. It was so easy to grab Gig, tug the sensitive little ballsac.

"Shan! Christ, man. That's hot."

"Mmm." Better. Still coherent, but better. Shannon went for more, his fingertips sliding along Gig's crease, where he tapped the tiny hole.

Gig pushed back against him, and man, he could feel the slide of skin on skin forever and never tire of it. "Want to fuck you, babe. Can I do that?"

"I sure as shit hope so."

"Ass. I mean do you want me to?"

"Shan." One of his hands was drawn to that perfect little bubble butt. "This is my ass."

Then Gig pressed close, lips to his ear. "Fuck me, man. Deep and hard. I've wanted you for years."

"Oh, God." Shannon nodded, panting hard, his chest heaving. Okay, lube. Gig was special and this was their first time -- spit wasn't gonna do it.

"What?" Gig was looking wild around the eyes. "What is it?"

"Shh. Chill. I got you." This was the Gig he knew, solid in emergency, a little wigged in the aftermath.

"You were all worried-looking." Gig grinned a little.

"I just need lube, baby." Shan stroked Gig's cheek. "Breathe."

Gig turned his head, lips wrapping around his fingers.

Electricity shot through his body, from his hand to his shoulder, then down. His dick jerked, and Shannon laughed. "Nice one."

God help him, he could get used to those smiles. He didn't know Gig had that much happy in him. Shannon knew it was for him, and he kissed Gig to show his pleasure at the thought.

Gig wrapped right around him again, sucking his tongue.

Distracting man. When Shannon broke for air this time he rolled away so he could get the damned lube. Gig's hands grabbed at his ass, squeezing good and hard. Turnabout was fair play, he guessed. Gig liked his ass just as much as he liked Gig's.

He focused on digging the lube out of his pack, and Gig? Gig seemed focused on licking the line of his spine. He wiggled, giving Gig some warning that he was turning around. "Coming back, baby."

Gig nodded and stretched out for him, compact and perfect. He loved all that pale skin, the tiny brown nipples. Shan rubbed one, nudging it and pushing it from side to side.

Moaning, Gig stretched out for him, giving him more to touch. He wanted to touch every inch -- from top to bottom. He licked his lips, then bent to nip at one bit of flesh. There was a scar tracing Gig's rib cage, the claw marks of a werewolf clear as day. Shannon frowned and licked his way down, loving on the skin. He remembered this one. Fucking beast had waited until they'd left Gig alone, then took him. Gig had kicked its ass.

His geek was tough as hell.

"You're in your head too much, Shan. Come back to me." Gig traced a scar on Shannon's cheek.

"Fuck yeah." Could'ves and should'ves had no place here. He grabbed the lube firmly and popped the top with his thumb, a trick he'd learned a long while back from Spider.

Time to play.

He pushed one finger in with little fanfare, slicked up and added another. He stretched that tight little hole, wanting Gig crazy for him. The sweet body gripped around his fingers, squeezing him tight. He pushed a little harder, needing to know Gig was good and stretched. No hurting.

"More. One more." Gig bent his leg, spread wider. Goddamn.

"I can do that, baby. I so can." He added a tiny bit more lube. Then he slid another finger in.

Oh, look at that. The sight of his fingers disappearing in the tiny hole fucking fascinated him. Shannon wanted to watch his dick in there, too, so he had to get the angle just right.

The thought had his fingers pushing deep and Gig arched, nodding furiously. "There!"

"Love how you look like this," Shannon said.

"Don't stop, huh? Need you like whoa."

"I hear you." Shannon knew he couldn't stop now if the mountain collapsed. Gig needed him and he wanted that sweet ass more than his next breath.

He pulled his fingers free so he could lube up his cock.

Gig's eyes burned, focused on him. The man watched him like he was Christmas morning. It was the hottest fucking thing since sliced bread. Well, he didn't like store-bought bread much, so maybe that was a bad analogy.

Shannon laughed when Gig slapped his belly. "Focus, Shan."

He grabbed his dick and pumped it. "Do I look less than focused on you, baby?"

"Yep. Pay attention." Gig grinned.

"I am, I swear. Your skin is so smooth. So hot. And your dick is amazing." He wasn't very good at this whole seduction thing, pretty words not coming easy to him.

"Come and fuck me, babe." Gig tugged at him, getting him settled between those spread legs. Shan found himself a little breathless, just the slightest bit overwhelmed. This was a longtime dream.

He gloved up, rubbed his cock against the tiny hole. Then he gritted his teeth and slid inside a scant inch. The ring of muscles rasped against his sensitive cockhead, the friction enough to make him stop and grit his teeth.

Tight. Jesus. Tight. He'd imagined this a million times, but this was better than anything. Gig's body was like a furnace inside and he worked himself in, centimeter by tortuous centimeter.

When his hips hit that fine ass, he stopped, breathing deep.

Jesus Christ, that was perfect.

Those dark eyes stared into his, Gig watching his every move. Shannon nodded because he knew what to do next. Move. He pulled out to where he almost lost that sweet sheath, then Shannon slammed in to the root.

Gig cried out, body bucking under him. He glanced down, watching his dick slide in and out, stretching the tiny hole.

"So fucking sexy, baby. I can't believe I finally get this." He sank in to the balls, moaning low.

"Shan. Oh, more." Gig was begging him now, touching him, fingers clumsy, little sparks flying through the air.

The tingling began to grow, settling deep in his balls. He grunted, gritting his teeth to hold back, wanting Gig to get there with him. Weird, because normally he didn't stress it, but Gig. Shit, he was special.

This could very well be the love of his life. How fucking weird was that?

Gig bared his teeth at Shannon. "Will you fuck me harder, damn it?"

"Bossy!" He swatted Gig's butt.

Gig hooted, and Shannon had never laughed during sex before, but he couldn't help himself. Gig made him fucking happy.

It was insane. Honestly. Wonderfully, amazingly insane.

"Love. Gig."

"Yeah. Harder." Gig reached up, cupped his cheek.

Shannon nodded, and finally gave up thinking for feeling, and the whole world went red-hot and sparkling. He thrust two, maybe three more times before he shot his seed deep in Gig's ass, his brain shorting out.

He reached for Gig's cock, discovering that his lover had spent. Damn. He'd have to make that up to the man later. By sucking him off and paying full attention.

"Oh, baby. You rock my world."

"Yeah. Yeah, that was... Damn, man."

"Was it?" He stared into Gig's eyes. "I didn't go too fast?"

Gig arched into him, rubbing them together and making them sticky. "This feel like I'm dissatisfied?"

"No." He grinned. "You feel amazing." In fact, Gig felt like heaven on earth.

Shannon had never thought he could find such happiness in a big cavern with a weird geek lover and a bunch of dragons. It just went to show how wrong a man could be, and how he had to accept his mistakes.

He and Gig were meant to be. It was just what it was. His team was family.

"Now all we have to do is make sure no one comes for the babies," Gig said. "Do you think it will work?"

"I think it has to."

"Okay." Gig snuggled, covering them with a blanket, and soon they had two baby dragons with them, purple and green. So sweet.

Gig's cheek was on his shoulder, Estrella was curled in the center of his chest. Shannon made a happy noise, glad that the battle was won for now and that his family was safe.

Hopefully, they would have plenty of time to figure out the rest.

Epilogue

I ce sat in the big bathing pool, so tickled with their week's work that he could hardly bear it.

Damien had closed the entrance with fire, melting the rock, leaving them the tiny exit in the rear of the mountain chamber, as well as the old cave exit Damien used. Keon was back to his normal, laughing self. He had his team.

Life was good.

Keon nudged Ice with his toes, breaking his thoughts. "Damien is talking to you, honey."

"Huh? Sorry, big guy. I was woolgathering. What's up?"

There are more. Damien's voice ran in his head.

Ice tried not to roll his eyes. Damien always sounded cryptic, like Yoda. "More what?"

Of us.

One image after another of winged dragons in the desert slipped into his brain. Like little Estrella. Desert? They were in the frozen north, after all. What kind of dragons lived in the heat?

They need help.

Ice glanced at Keon, who smiled and spread his hands, saying, "I don't know how he knows, but he always does."

Damien huffed a hot breath. *My job.*

"I thought your job was to be brushed…" Keon teased.

Brushing. Damien's eyes closed at the thought, the big dragon's expression like a smile. *Chino. His bonded waits for him.*

Where, beloved? Keon's voice was fond, so happy. The dragons were safe, and Ice had found that let Keon be at peace.

In the place below where Ice comes from. Where it's hot and dry.

Mexico, eh? Interesting.

Keon nodded. "It's a place to start."

"I'll tell Chino when we're done bathing."

"Later." Keon encouraged, and reached for him with one hand.

Ice nodded, letting his body slide closer to his lover's, his smile no longer surprising him. "Definitely later."

"Much later."

Damien chuckled. *Silly children.*

Ice laughed, and Keon kissed the sound away. Damien might make fun, but he was a happy dragon with a bunch of people to protect his brood of younglings.

Ice figured that meant life was pretty good for the big guy, too. All around, the Elemental Ops team was starting a whole new chapter in their lives.

Author's note:

The Elemental Ops story actually began at the end of a series called Mixed Breeds. While all of the El Ops books are m/m, Mixed Breeds included menages. Damon, or Spider, from the Elemental Ops team gets a man and a women as his new lovers. While it's not mandatory to understand El Ops, and has no dragons in the tale, I thought you might like to read how it all began.

XXOO

Julia T.

Hunted

Chapter One

Chase watched the crowd, his red Solo cup held loosely in his left hand. He was hunting tonight, and his target had just shown up. The lady in question had curves to spare, wrapped in a sweet little sundress, her legs showed off perfectly by a pair of strappy heels. Her deep chestnut hair was pulled back, letting her gold earrings dance against the skin of her shoulders.

Definitely a kitty of some sort.

He glanced at his watch. His friend Jason should be here soon to introduce them. Chase lived in Boulder, so he rarely got to meet the shifters in Denver. Jason knew everyone.

The prey slipped between two burly bear shifters to get to the bar, and she got a real glass, not a silly red plastic thing. He guessed that was the difference between cheap beer and a fancy cocktail.

Lord, he hated these mixer meetup things. They weren't for speed dating. They were for getting to know the other shifters in the area. Their kind was being hunted, and there was safety in numbers. Still, he sat there with his nose twitching, wanting to growl, knowing he had to behave. It was a tough thing.

He checked his watch again. Damn it, where was Jason? Some asshole was making the move on his girl, and Chase didn't want to have to go beat the man down.

Whoa. Huh. *His* girl?

"You look constipated," Jason said into his ear, making him jump.

"Thanks, asshole." Really, why was he friends with this guy?

"No problem. You know, I really should have brought Rita. They're the ones who are friends."

"Where are Scott and Rita?" Last year Jason had hooked up with not one but two other shifters. A fox and a coyote.

"Scott was feeling under the weather, so Rita stayed home with him." Jason winked. Yeah, Scott hated these shifter mixers more than Chase did. Under the weather, his ass.

"Well, thanks for coming out, man."

"Anything if it will help with the hunters," Jason said firmly, mouth pressing into a thin line.

Chase nodded soberly. Jason had lost someone dear to him to hunters, and had almost not taken the chance on love again. He was glad his friend had moved on. Chase liked Rita and Scott both.

"Introduce us before that jerk makes any more of a play for her?"

Jason glanced at him, raising a brow. "Oh, growly."

"She's special." He didn't know what it was about this one, but Chase wanted her to himself.

Grinning, Jason nodded and started toward Miss Slinky Kitty. "She is. I'm glad you see it."

"I think everyone does." Two more men were circling her like buzzards, waiting for their turn.

"Good thing I know her," Jason said before elbowing in next to the lady in question. "Excuse me. Hi, Shanna."

"Jason!" Shanna beamed at Jason, taking his arm. "Good to see you. Where's my girl?" She peered around the room, clearly looking for Rita.

"She had to take care of a very pouty Scott. Good to see you, too." Jason drew Shanna away from her admirers. "I have someone I want you to meet."

"Oh? Are you getting into matchmaking now?"

"No."

Chase snorted. Jason had met both his lovers on a blind date. The same blind date. He wasn't one to take a chance on doing that to someone else, thank God.

Shanna glanced at Chase, pursing her lips. "Hi."

"Hi," Chase said, holding out a hand. "Chase Montgomery."

"Shanna Eli. Nice to meet you."

They shook hands, her pink-manicured nails oddly delicate against his rough skin. He was glad Jason was there, because she probably wouldn't have given him the time of day if he'd gone it alone. As it was, the touch jolted him all the way up his arm, making his scalp prickle. "You, too. I asked Jason to introduce us because he says you're good at what you do."

She tilted her head. Shanna had an expressive face, her eyebrows moving up and down. "Am I?"

Jason chuckled. "Like viciously. She's way more dangerous than she looks."

"Mmm. She looks pretty dangerous." Chase let himself admire a little. She was stacked to the ceiling, this lady. He could get lost in those curves for days.

"You have no idea." Her eyes fascinated him, and how weird was that? He wasn't looking to get laid.

No, he was looking to do his job. Fix the hunter thing. Chase smiled. "Do you have a moment?"

"Sure. Walk with me." She looked over his shoulder. "Jason, get me something fizzy and non-alcoholic."

It wasn't a request. She was damned forceful. The way Jason trotted off to do her bidding amazed him.

Chase walked with her, having to try too hard to keep his hands to himself. He wanted to touch her ass. Badly. She smelled amazing, cinnamon and ginger and gun oil?

Gun oil? Maybe she was as dangerous as Jason said. He put his hands in his pockets and waited for her to start.

"So, tell me, why do you need a PI?"

He moved a little closer so he didn't have to raise his voice over the music. "Hunters. You've heard about the situation, yeah?"

"A bit, yes." Her eyes narrowed, nose wrinkling so quickly that he almost missed it.

"Well, the whole thing is causing issues, especially in the pack. Folks are getting paranoid. Insular. Vigilante-ism isn't far off. I've been tasked with finding the source."

"And you think I'll be useful because?"

"Because you're more familiar with the outlying areas than I am. You have more connections because you're not pack-specific. You're not bound by pack rules so I don't have to spend more time protecting you than working with you." He ticked all the things off on his fingers.

"True. Is there going to be cash involved in it? Not that I'm mercenary, but…" She grinned. "Well, a girl's got to keep herself in shoes."

"I'll pay your standard fee, yeah. I wanted to meet you here, though. Not at your office."

"Wanted to meet me on neutral ground?" Those eyebrows went up and down again.

"Well, that, and I didn't want the pack following me or hunters watching." This was a safe place, or at least safer than most. They had anonymity and numbers.

"Ah… Are you cheating on your alpha?" She stepped closer, let him scent her.

"Nope." Chase lifted his chin, knowing she'd want to test him as well. "I'm here on his orders, just on the QT. There's a lot of unrest."

"That happens when you're flushed out of the trees by assholes on four wheelers." She brushed her hand over her collarbone and moved the neckline of her dress, exposing a circular scar that was an abomination on the porcelain skin.

"Shit. No wonder Jason thought you'd help me." She'd been hunted firsthand. "What can you tell me about them?"

"They're human, well-equipped, definitely well-organized. Don't think too well on their feet, though."

"So, they're foot soldiers." Not a surprise, but good to know. If they floundered under lack of leadership, then he just needed to take off the head of the organization. The rest would slowly disappear.

"They think we're contagious. Assholes. Good shots, though, at least mid-range. They don't go for groups of us, not yet, but I think it's coming." Her words were emotionless, clipped. "Do you have a plan?"

"I have an idea. Which is not as good as a plan." Pack resources were limited. He and the alpha, Lance, were doing this out of their own pockets and on their own time. The need for action was getting urgent, though. Things were about to turn into one of those bad movies where werebeasts and humans squared off.

"No, but it's better than nothing, which is what everyone else has, apparently."

"That's it. But now I have new information, too. I think we need to hunt a little on our own. Track one of these guys down."

"I'll see what I can do, what I can find out."

Like she hadn't been looking. There was no way someone hurt her that bad and she wasn't going to hunt them down and hurt them.

"We either need to shoot high or isolate someone new, someone who will crack and give us information. I just need to know where to start." He'd been protecting the alpha for a while as a full-time job; he was a little out of touch.

She nodded, painted lips pursing again. "Like I said, I'll get hold of you if I find something worth your cash. You have a number?"

He did, and she had to have a lead. He could see it in the way her eyebrows drew together instead of going up.

"I even have a check," Chase said.

"Cash is better, but I like a man who will pay upfront."

"I thought you'd enjoy that." He passed it to her, along with his card.

"Thank you." The papers disappeared. "I'll make sure to check in, when I have information to share."

"You can call any time." Was he flirting? He thought he was. Now that the business was done. For the moment. God, he was an idiot.

She laughed, gave him a once-over, like she was looking at him for the first time. Maybe she was. She was professional, so she'd only been seeing him as a job. "It's tempting."

"Good. I like pho." He hoped she did, too. What wasn't to like about rice noodles, broth and rare beef?

"Are you asking me to supper?" she said, her grin widening.

"I am. There's a place called Saigon Palace not far from here."

"I don't usually date clients, but I'm not at work, am I?" She raised one shoulder, her breasts shifting under the cloth.

"Neither am I." He glanced around. "This *is* a mixer."

Her laugh was husky, pure sex. "A chance to whirl around the bowl together?"

Grinning, he nodded. "Like a big old pot. Pho would be way better."

"I can handle that. You, me, noodles…" Her head tilted, nose wrinkling up. "You hear that?"

He stopped, ears perked. There was a hum, an odd buzz like a swarm of bees. It was strange. Electric. "Yeah. Yeah, I do." He sniffed hard, trying to detect any hint of scent to connect to the sound.

"I don't like it." She started moving toward the gate, and no one should move in heels like they were running shoes.

He caught a whiff of acrid smoke and started chasing her, knowing he needed to get between all these shifters and whatever it was coming after them.

Shanna lost her shoes just before she leapt, landing on the top of the stone wall, Glock in hand. Shit, he didn't even know where she'd hidden that. He drew his own weapon, switching off the safety. She fired off three rounds, and they were quiet, quick, suppressed shots that no one noticed over the din of music and laughter.

He heard a muted shout of surprise, a scuffling of booted feet. Someone hadn't expected his girl.

Three more shots and she leapt, disappearing on the other side of the wall.

Crap. He found a place to scramble over the wall, feeling utterly useless. Like bad backup in a terrible cop movie.

What he saw was two men, down and still on the ground, a third with the barrel of a gun pressed to his forehead. Shanna looked over at him, green eyes lit from within, her pride obvious. "This enough of a lead, pup?"

"Yeah." Chase grinned, feeling a feral surge of triumph. "Yeah, I think that'll do."

Damon couldn't fucking believe he'd gotten caught. By one of them. A woman. Jesus, he was like a rank amateur. Or maybe the guys he worked with were that stupid, getting them noticed. How the hell had he gotten talked into this anyway?

Oh, yeah. Patriotism. The root of all evil.

He was sitting in the back of the most uncomfortable car in the history of sports cars, zip-tied so tight that his fingers and feet were numb, a growly asshole holding a pistol on him while the hottest chick he ever saw drove.

He'd made the mistake once of asking a question. Mr. Growly had smacked him. With the barrel of the gun, leaving blood trickling down his cheek.

They headed out of the suburbs and up into the mountains. There was no way -- no way -- this muscle car was going to take the hills. It didn't have enough weight in its back end. When she wiped out he'd make a run for it. In the meantime, he guessed he should consider himself lucky that he was mobile. He was the one with the tranq gun, so he'd stayed awake.

"Where are you going, honey?" big and growly asked.

"To switch out vehicles and put on a pair of jeans," she said. "I want my Jeep."

Damn. That meant the lady lived up this way. So much for wrecking the car. If she was familiar with the area, she would get them there.

Damon tried to loosen the cuffs, tried to get some breathing room. They were plastic riot cuffs, and not letting up a bit. He didn't have enough… heat built up to melt them, either.

"Don't bother." Her eyes met his in the rear view. "You're not going anywhere. Don't be an idiot and waste your energy. You'll need it."

"What for? Are we playing football later?" Damon asked, trying for a cocky grin.

"Oh, honey, we're playing a much better game. It's called Make the Asshole Spill His Guts." Her smile was pure ice.

"Yeah? This guy going to show you his intestines?" He nodded at gun-toting man.

"That depends on whether he makes good with his promise of Vietnamese food."

"Are we really going to tell him where we're going to dinner?" The guy could growl. Really, really. Impressive.

"There is more than one pho place in Denver, pup, and I'm going to kill him, so it really doesn't matter."

"Oh, killing isn't necessary." Damon hadn't been planning on killing anyone in the raid. Just taking a prisoner or two. Not the shifter kind, either. No, the assholes he was working with were really his target.

"No? You've killed enough of my kind, his kind. It seems more than fair." She spun off the main road, her tires spinning.

Damon wasn't given to babbling, but he thought at this point he might point out a pertinent fact. "Hey, this was my first raid. I haven't killed anyone." Not of their kind, anyway. He'd done his share of Black Ops.

"Then you are one unlucky bastard." She wheeled into a nearly invisible dirt road, managing to make the drive without hitting a single fucking bump. Damn it. Her territory. Maybe he needed to work on the man with the gun instead.

"You're drilling a hole in my head, man." It was totally going to leave a mark.

"Am I? Shame." The barrel did back off, though, the barest bit.

Bingo. The guy was less of a hardass. Hot, too. Not quite as hot as the chick, who had this slinky, dangerous vibe, but the pale hair and almost golden eyes went well with the guy's broad shoulders and tanned skin.

They pulled up into a clearing, a gorgeous little cabin sitting there with a trashed Jeep parked outside. The guy gave the chick a look, eyebrows raised, and she shrugged. "Work truck."

"Come on, you." Gun boy poked him again, and nodded at the door, then opened it for him.

Damon pushed his way out and on his feet. The strips around his ankles let him walk, kind of. Shuffle. Stumble. He was getting fucking sick of this. Damon wasn't used to feeling clumsy.

"Bring him onto the porch. I'm not dressed for torture." The lady climbed the stairs to the porch, her ass like a wet dream.

"There's no torture here. I'm just in it for the money, man." Damon met her stare with his. "And because they said you were freaks. Hey, a guy's gotta eat."

"So you're just a paid killer. No offense."

"None taken. If you're listening, though, I had a tranq gun. No killing with that." Sheesh she was dense. And he was losing his powers of persuasion with the fairer sex, damn it.

"A tranq gun. Right." The blow to his jaw was so fast he never saw it coming. "Liar."

"No, he did have a tranq." The growly guy frowned. "I

thought that was why he stayed upright."

"He stayed upright because we needed one to question."

The guy pursed his lips. "He seems to be talking pretty well."

"Whose side are you on? They're killing us!" She stomped her foot -- her bare foot, fuck, she'd caught him in bare feet? -- and growled. "I'm not one hundred percent sure drugging one of us to keep and experiment on is preferable to murder!"

"No. I get that." Growly sighed, rolling his head on his neck. "I'm all for eliminating a threat." The guy sneered at him. "I'm just not sure he's a threat."

"Seriously? You're going to have a pissing contest with a guy in cuffs?" Damon raised a brow. He had to get free from this, goddamn it.

"No, asshole, I'm having a pissing contest with her." The guy jerked his thumb at hot woman. "You know what, honey, have at him."

One of those Glocks came up, fast and sure, not wavering a bit. "Tell me who you are."

"Jon Doe." That would be true enough if they killed him. His past had been carefully erased by his employer. The US government was good at wet work, and Damon had been doing it a long time.

"Jon Doe. Chase, just kill him and take me to supper."

Damon glanced at Chase, gauging the man's willingness to do exactly that. Damn. The fool's eyes lit up.

He decided to throw them a bone. "Chase must be hungry. I'm Damon. Ex black ops."

"So what did we do to deserve hunting?" God, she had the most amazing eyes. Okay, stop it. This chick was not for playing with. Even if her threatening was more erotic than most women's flirting.

"They say you're contagious."

"Bullshit." Both of them spoke together.

He knew that, but he had to act like he didn't. So he stared. The government was fully aware that they were relatively harmless, these shifter folks. That was why Damon was supposed to infiltrate the hunter cell and bring them down.

"What? You think if we were that there wouldn't be millions of us? Are you stupid?" Her eyes were glowing. *Glowing*. Nothing he'd seen in his supposed training had prepared him for her having that kind of power.

"Do you have a cage, honey?" Now the Chase guy sounded amused.

"A cage?" She turned to Chase, the motion sensual as fuck, her interest in the big guy clear.

"Yeah. I say we bite him and toss him in there. Go to supper. He'll see that we're not a disease." Chase eyed him like he was a big steak. Okay, time to get the heat building up.

Damon started stoking his internal fire as best he could in the cool mountain air.

"Works for me. We can lock him in the shed," the lady murmured, looking all too pleased with the idea.

"Good deal."

No. No way. He was not getting bit. Damon started struggling, wiggling across the floor where they'd pushed him down like a worm on a hook. He'd seen all the literature on these guys. They weren't contagious, but animal bites could get infected.

"Let me go get some jeans on and the key. I'll be right back."

"We'll be right here." One of Chase's feet landed on Damon's hip, holding him down when he'd almost made the edge of the porch.

"I'm not a fucking murderer, man."

"No?" Chase put a little more pressure into holding him down. "You have a full dose of stupid."

"I have a full dose of need to pay the rent, man." He would rather let them believe he was in it for the money than let on the truth. They didn't need to know what was going on. He had his orders.

"My heart bleeds for you."

"I can tell." Damon worked at the damned cuffs, hoping to

heat the plastic up enough to bend it. He just wasn't hot enough yet.

"I just don't get it. We're not hurting anyone. We've had the packs here for generations."

"I don't make the rules." He really, really needed to be loose. This tied up thing wasn't working.

"The eternal call of idiot soldiers. I was just following orders." Okay, she looked better in jeans than in a fancy dress. Her ass looked luscious, round and firm.

"That's me. Idiot. Come on, lady, let me go."

"Not an option." She growled softly, yanking him up to a standing position. "Come on. Barn."

"Biting me would be a very bad idea." God knew what it would do to his body chemistry. He had a delicate enough balance as it was, despite his hard-won buff body.

"Why?" Her head tilted. "Are you contagious? Humans?"

"You never know." He wasn't contagious. He didn't think. Hell, no one had ever bitten him hard enough to find out.

"Oh, I've fucked humans, Shanna. You just have to be gentle with them, but they're not contagious."

"Good to know."

They were comedians. Great. "You two should take your act on the road," Damon said.

"Good idea. Up." Chase hauled Damon around, and Shanna shoved him. His cuffed feet weren't up to the speed of the movement and Damon started to topple over.

They caught him, both of them strong, and the burn in the base of his brain responded, his skin beginning to tingle with heat. Shit, what the hell was that? Whatever it was, it was more dangerous than any weapon, and Damon struggled.

"Easy, easy." Chase sounded worried. "What the fuck? Shanna?"

"I don't know." Her nose brushed across his cheek. "Whoa."

"Yeah. Let me go and I won't do it again." Damon was tossing out anything, desperate.

"Shut up," Shanna growled, letting Chase carry him so she could unlock the shed. "Inside."

They put him on a lawn chair, two pairs of eyes glowing at him in the dark, that animal shine fascinating. He pressed back, feeling the danger of this whole thing keenly. When they advanced, he kicked out, trying one last-ditch effort to keep those teeth away from his skin.

"You're not one of us." Shanna's voice was pure growl, and so was Chase's when he answered her.

"He's not one of them, either, though. No. He's something else." Chase tilted his head. "I don't know what."

She looked at him, lips twisting. "So, what are you? And don't lie."

He stared at her, trying for deadpan. "US government property."

"What do they want with us?"

He blew out a deep breath. Now he was in deep, but they knew something was off about him. Might as well see if the truth worked. "We don't want you. We want the hunters."

"Honey…" Shanna looked at him, head tilted. "I hate to be the one to break the news, but you were running with them. The hunters. The ones with the big guns."

Damon rolled his eyes. "Look, do you get pizza delivery up here? I'll buy, we'll talk. It'll be great."

"God, I wish." For the first time, she was a real girl, someone human, rolling her eyes and licking her lips.

"Seriously?" The Chase guy was grinning, though. "Well, if we're gonna eat with this guy, tell me you have the stuff to make waffles. Since we can't have pizza or pho."

This? Was surreal. Bizarre. Entertaining as hell.

"We have to keep him tied up. Do you cook waffles?" Shanna asked.

"I do. With bacon. If you have bacon."

Damon snorted. "I like bacon."

"Everyone likes bacon." She looked between them, unsure.

"Fuck it," Chase said. "This has been the weirdest night ever. We can tie him to the chair. Come on."

Well, being dragged into the house was better than in the barn about to be gnawed on. He might even get a waffle out of it.

Chapter Two

Somehow, Shanna had lost control here.

She had dealt with males -- lots of them. Big ones. Growly ones. Ones that played with guns. None of them had made her so fucking confused as these two comedians.

They ended up in her kitchen, the big, dark hunter calling himself Damon tied to her chair. She had this terrible urge to climb on him and ride, which was ridiculous. She didn't fuck humans. Ever. That always ended up biting her on the ass, making her feel like a bitch for hiding half her life from them.

Then there was Chase, big and golden and lovely. He was making waffle batter out of her gluten free Bisquick. This was insane. He kept looking at her like she was edible, like he could lick her, top to bottom.

"Oh, stop it."

Damon looked at her, eyebrows arched. "What?"

"Nothing."

Chase grinned before rooting through her cabinets. "No maple?"

"It's in the fridge."

"Oh, cool. Do you like sweet? I know some, uh…" Chase glanced at Damon. "A friend of mine doesn't."

"I like it." Some cat shifters couldn't taste sweet at all, but she could, thank the moon.

"Oh, good." He was cooking a metric ton of bacon in her toaster oven. It smelled wonderful, smoky, rich. Oh, for God's sake.

"We brought you in. You're supposed to be explaining." She needed to take control of the situation, starting with Damon.

He just nodded, eyes on her boobs, which she had pushed up by folding her arms over her chest. Men.

"Okay," Damon shifted, wincing, but she wasn't going to fall for the feel sorry for me ploy. "I'm supposed to be infiltrating the hunters' organization. I was doing great."

"Uh-huh. Infiltrating. Like a super spy."

"I was!" He looked so affronted. "I'm good at what I do. I was on my first raid. I was supposed to get an idea of their procedures."

She looked at Chase. How was she supposed to know what the truth was?

Chase shrugged, checking the waffle iron. "I don't know, honey. Who would make up a story like this?"

"Who would pretend to kill folks for fun?"

"I didn't kill anyone!" Damon could growl a little. Impressive. Not like her or Chase, or better yet, her bear friend Zane.

"I did." She was one hell of a shot, and she knew it.

"Yeah, well, I had the tranq just for them, in case they got lucky and found your party." Damon paused, frowning. "Which they did."

"Indeed. How did that happen?" If it was one of their own giving them up, there would be hell to pay. Not everyone had a pack structure like Chase's wolves, but the community was relatively small.

"That I don't know. I haven't figured out where they get their intel."

God, she had a headache. The tightness started right across her shoulders and up over her scalp, all tension. She should have gone to Estes with her sisters. Then she could have avoided both these asshats. Beautiful, dangerous asshats.

Chase's hands landed on her shoulders, surprising the fuck out of her. She jumped half a foot.

"Damn, you're tense," he murmured, digging his thumbs in.

Oh, God, he had good hands, wide and strong, the touch giving her goosebumps.

No relaxing. No relaxing. Damn, that was so good. Her head fell forward, and she closed her eyes. She wanted to moan, but she wasn't going to. That would give Chase too much satisfaction.

That tingling came again, and she swore it came from Damon, in waves. She opened her eyes to stare, only to find him giving her an equally baffled look. It wasn't a hallucination, though, her nerves were tingling.

"What is that?" Chase asked. "That buzz?"

"I don't know. It's him."

They both glanced at Damon, who actually pulled back as much as he could, tied as he was. "I didn't do it."

"It's you." And Shanna thought he knew it. He was lying to them about something.

"Nope. No buzzing. I'm just a dude." He batted his long, black lashes.

She growled and pounced, landing in the man's lap, going eye to eye with him. "Quit lying!"

"You have me tied to a chair!" He growled every word, right there, so close his lips brushed hers.

"What *are* you?" She was vibrating, shivering with the waves of… whatever the fuck it was… pouring off him. He was electric, and hot as fire. She put her hand over his heart, and the odd beat was definitely not human.

Chase came up behind her, body against her back, hand covering hers on Damon's chest, and she gasped, feeling like lightning had struck.

"Christ, are you two trying to electrocute me?"

"Us?"

Chase growled. "It's you."

Damon struggled to throw her off. "Trust me, I don't shoot sparks. I just… warm things up from time to time."

"Warm things up." She was warm. Christ, she was melted and wet and so fucking turned on it couldn't be real. It had to be something like a pheromone or a chemical the government cooked up. That was why he was really here, right?

"Uh-huh." Chase's mouth was on the back of her neck, lips wet and soft, cock hard on the small of her back.

This was the craziest thing ever. When Chase leaned one hand on Damon's shoulder, she almost came; the three of them touching too damned much to bear.

"What the fuck…" Damon's head fell back, Adam's apple bobbing, and Shanna had to lean forward, teeth on his skin. He tasted like fire, like the best kind of smoky yumminess.

"God. This is nuts." Chase rubbed against her like he was the cat.

"You can't bite on me."

"Not biting hard." She did though. She bit down hard enough to break the skin.

The feeling was like biting a live wire. Her nipples throbbed, her cunt clenching. She squeezed her thighs around his. Chase jerked against her back.

She heard Chase groan, and then the wolf was taking Damon's lips, biting and licking, demanding a kiss. The electricity between them flared a notch higher. If they got any more going on, she was going up in flames.

Somehow she was grinding, rocking between them, her thighs screaming. Her breasts bounced, rubbing Damon's chest, making her gasp.

The man reached for her, grabbed her hips and pulled her closer.

Wait. How did his hands get free? Chase hadn't let him go. What was that smoldering smell? She pulled back, bumping Chase in the chest. The riot cuffs lay on the floor, neatly burned in half. The ones on his feet were gone, too.

"Don't," Damon said, yanking her back in for another kiss. He kissed like he was pure flame, and she twisted, begging for more. Chase joined in, the man leaning over her, hands sliding around to cover her breasts.

She jerked, her belly feeling so tight that it ached. This was a bad idea. Terrible. She wanted them like she'd never wanted anything in her life.

When Damon surged to his feet, carrying her and Chase both backward with the momentum, she clung to him, crying out.

"Bed, lady. Now."

"What?" No. No, she didn't do this. This was not how this worked. She was in control. "Last door on the right."

"Thank God," Chase murmured, tugging her into his arms and carrying her down the hall.

Both men were rubbing, bouncing off the walls and tearing at clothes. She got Damon's black T-shirt off, nails digging into the smooth, tanned skin. His broad chest and flat, brown nipples begged for scratching, touching. Chase was leaner, his skin paler, dusted with golden hair.

They burst into her bedroom, and Chase growled, the sound vibrating against her back. "Fuck. Smell you here. Heaven."

No one had ever told her that before, not even the few male cats she'd been with.

Damon pulled her top off, groaning as her body came into view. "Bra, man. The hooks. Please. I gotta taste."

"Yeah. Yeah." Chase hunted the hooks on her back, but smart boy that he was, he realized her plunge bra had one clasp in the front. "Real observant, dude."

"Fuck you." Damon groaned and lifted her, lips wrapping around one nipple. Shanna arched, trusting in Chase to keep her upright.

Those strong arms wrapped around her, one under her breasts, pushing them up for Damon. These two men worked together like a well-oiled machine. Damon's lips pulled firmly, the suction hard and steady, like the man was starving for her. Every single suck tugged at her clit, making her legs tingle.

Chase was so hard against her ass, his cock poking and poking. This was completely out of control. They were on fire, and for a moment she smelled brimstone and thought that was not just a phrase.

"Need." Chase bit her shoulder, teeth digging in.

"Yes." She let her head fall back, let Damon have at her neck.

She heard the button of her jeans ping off the wall somewhere. Damn. She liked those jeans. It was worth it to have nothing but bare skin between her and Damon, though where his clothes had gone she had no idea. His cock slid against her folds, and she yowled softly, arching to take him in.

"I can help," Chase said, sliding his fingers down her belly to her cunt. He separated her, opening her up for Damon.

"Owe you, man." Damon arched up and she took him, all the way to the root.

"Uh-huh. You so do. Gonna make you get me off."

Her pussy clenched at the idea of her two boys touching each other, hands and mouths on cocks.

Damon grunted, slamming up into her. "Fuck. Fuck, yeah."

"God, you two are pretty. So hot." Chase worked her clit, right there, his knuckles dragging on Damon's skin.

Hot was right. She was burning up, driving herself on that amazing cock, those quick, smart fingers. The men were inside her, all around her and their scents were perfect.

She arched, clenching her fingers into a fist. "Fuck! Don't stop."

"Not stopping. Come on, girl. On my prick," Damon grated out.

She rode him up and down, just rocking and rolling. The bed sang, their bodies slapping together. Chase felt like heaven, and Damon felt like all the good things that sent you to hell.

Someone's hands were on her ass, someone's were on her breasts, and she was going to scream. Damon thrust up hard, slamming into her, and Chase held her down so all she could do was grind.

The orgasm built, climbing up through her body, setting her alight. Damon's skin felt like he might start steaming any moment, his cock an iron rod inside her. They were determined to work together to get her to come. She screamed when it let go, sensation rocking her body, muscle spasms rocking her pussy.

Her head lolled on her neck when the orgasm ended, her whole body feeling lax.

"Christ. Need." Chase rolled off to one side of her and Damon, jacking his cock madly. Damon grabbed at Chase, and the two men slammed together, Shanna curling on one side to watch.

The kiss looked painful, all teeth and power. They grappled, finally ending up stroking each other. Chase was all growls and deep rumbles, Damon's skin was red, heat pouring off him. They worked their arms in a distinct rhythm, pulling each other hard. So perfectly male.

She reached out, fingers trailing along their sides, touching them both, and it was like lightning striking. They jerked, both of them moaning, turning toward her.

"Help us, honey."

Her fingers joined theirs, moving over their cocks. Fuck, that was hot. Literally as well as figuratively. She thought Damon might burn her. What the hell was he? Besides beautiful.

She crawled over them, straddling their thighs as they spread out for her. The three of them sort of melted together, hands and mouths moving, finding all the good spots. The boys touched each other and her, hands seemingly everywhere.

Chase and Damon shared one wild kiss after another, and fuck, had anything ever been so hot? She lost her train of thought, stilling her hands while she watched.

Slowly they turned to look at her, like they were of one mind, and she damn near melted. They moved like one man, closing in on her, Chase sliding between her legs, Damon pushing up behind Chase.

"Need you, kitten. Now." Chase ducked his head, lips catching one of her nipples and tugging.

"Sensitive." She was, too, from her breasts to her pussy. "I can take it, though."

"Oh, God. Good." Chase pushed inside her, wider than Damon but not as hot.

He curled over her, mouth everywhere, lips taunting her skin, dragging on her. He was beautiful, all golden hair and skin. Damon's knees brushed her legs, and she could feel his cock sliding between Chase's legs.

She couldn't believe this, couldn't believe that they would fall together like this so fast and easy. She panted, reached up, petting whoever she could reach. Shanna wrapped her legs around Chase, her heels kicking Damon's hips.

"Easy. Easy. Fuck, you two are a wildfire."

Damon's words made her eyes cross. Seriously? Burn Boy thought they were hot?

Chase laughed, staring down at her. "He's like an open flame and he says that?"

"Exactly." She pushed up, took herself a hot, hungry kiss. Chase opened up to her, then pushed back, his tongue in her mouth.

They rutted, all of them slamming together violently. God, she hoped her bed could take it. She hoped her body could take it. She was so wet, so open, but she was gonna be sore for sure.

Chase growled, teeth on her shoulder, shaking her a bit. Damon's hand flew, popping Chase's ass. "Be careful with her."

"Oh, fuck." Chase arched, cock slamming into her, his whole body shaking. Her cunt clenched down around him. That was the single sexiest thing she'd ever seen.

"Shanna. Guys." The words were bitten off, Chase's eyes glowing, hungry. "Please."

"What do you need, honey?" She stroked his cheek. "You want him to do it again?"

"I…"

Oh, fuck. Hot. She looked into Damon's eyes, nodded. There wasn't any room for shame. That could come later when they all realized what they'd done.

Damon smacked Chase again, then again, just driving them

all faster. Her second orgasm was barreling down like a Mack truck on a mountain pass. Chase fucked her like a madman, and she could feel Damon, hard, right there. He must be about to burst.

"Soon." She bit the word out, baring her teeth. "Soon, boys."

Chase nodded fiercely, his balls slapping her with each thrust. "Please. Soon."

Damon slammed them together. "Now."

She grunted, her next scream caught in her throat. Chase howled just like the wolf he was, his hips slapping her ass one last time.

Okay. Whoa. Also, wow. And vaguely, eek, with an emphasis on bone-melting. Even more so when Damon came for them, painting both of them with his seed. Jesus, he was frickin' tropical. Strong, too, as he lifted both of them off the bed when he reared back.

She stared at Chase, who stared back. Shit. What were they supposed to do now?

Damon dropped them back on the bed and collapsed next to them. "Damn. Yeah. You guys charged me up for days."

"Charged up. What does that mean?"

Damon glanced at her, sighing. "I don't suppose we can nap before I tell you my life story?"

"Demanding asshole!" Shanna shook her head.

Chase snorted. "We're boys. We come and snooze."

She pushed up on her elbows. "Promise me you won't run off. We need to know what's going on here." Shanna didn't just mean the hunter situation.

"You can stay right on top of me, keep me here." Cocky fucker.

Chase grinned at her, pulling her over so they could land on Damon. "Puppy pile!"

Shanna rolled her eyes, but allowed herself to be snuggled. At this rate, though, she was never going to get supper.

Chase woke up to a rumbling belly. Not his.

Shanna's.

Damn, someone needed food. He was reluctant to let go of either her or Damon, but someone needed to see if the waffle maker turned itself off.

It must have, right? Or else the smell would be horrendous. He removed himself from the pile of flesh and stretched, shaking his head. He wasn't sure what had happened, but he wasn't one to question his instincts too much.

He licked his lips, gaze dragging over them both. Yummy.

Oh, food. They needed food. He would rescue what he could of the waffles and stuff. He trotted to the kitchen, put the bacon back on and added more water and mix to the bowl. It was rescueable.

Woo. Cooking he could do without thinking, so he let his mind wander to the smokin' hot pair in the bedroom.

He knew he wanted her, but Damon? Usually there was some posturing, some feeling each other out with dudes. Okay, there was usually him on top. He'd never bottomed right up like that. In fact, he never even thought about it.

Maybe it was because Damon wasn't a wolf… Whatever it was, the man was electric. Amazing.

Chase loaded breakfast on a fancy tray he found under a cabinet. She had an amazing kitchen, clean and well-stocked with about a thousand small appliances. He loved it. The coffee was good stuff, too. The tray looked and smelled delicious, if he did say so himself.

Shanna's eyes opened when he came in, her nostrils flaring. "Butter."

"Bacon," Damon said, not opening his eyes.

"Uh-huh." Shanna nuzzled Damon. "Maple syrup."

"Yep. Are we going to eat or are you two going to have sex while pondering eating?" Either way, he could be happy.

"Food." Her eyes popped open, so bright. "I'm starving."

"Me too." Chase plopped down on the bed, putting down his

tray where it would balance.

Damon chuckled. "I could eat. Something small, maybe a water buffalo."

"Well, I got a stack of waffles and meat." He waved at the platter.

They all fell on the food like a pack, happy moans and low growls on the air. Huh. They were like a pack, weird as it was. He was already feeling so protective of them.

A piece of bacon was fed to him, and he finished it, nibbled on Shanna's fingers. Damon snuggled up close to him, pouring maple syrup on a plate of pancakes.

"I want a bite." Shanna leaned against him, lips open.

"Here." He fed her a not too delicate bite, watching her lick the fork with interest. She had the most luscious lips, like strawberry jam.

Damon swooped in, took her mouth in a hard kiss, before leaning back and grinning. "Yummy."

She blinked at them, lips swollen. "Uh. Yes."

Chase laughed. Distracted and flustered was a good look for her. He'd bet it was as unaccustomed to her as bottoming was to him.

She swatted at him. "Laughing at me!"

"I am. I can't help it." He was weirdly bubbly inside.

They started in on the bacon, biting and nibbling. Chase was jonesing on the little electric shocks popping off Damon. The man's skin felt amazing, almost like there was a buzz underneath.

"So, what are you?" he asked, nibbling a bite Shanna fed him.

"What are you two?" Damon responded. Little fuck, avoiding the question. Well, Damon wasn't little, but still.

"He's a puppy." Shanna was so helpful.

Two could play that game. "She's a puss," Chase said.

"Meow." She scraped her nails down his chest, making him yelp.

"Tooth and claw, you two." Damon shifted, making the bed dip. "I'm not sure what you'd call me. The government classifies me as a physical energy manipulator."

"Ooh. Sparky. Can you set shit on fire?" He loved this kind of thing. Loved it.

"Sometimes. I mean, I'm not Drew Barrymore." Damon grinned at him.

"Damn it. Drew Barrymore would mean more boob for me." He had to tease. Had to.

"You got plenty right there." Damon reached over and tweaked Shanna's left nipple. She'd been eating all the bacon and watching them like a fan at a tennis match.

Oh, didn't that make her nipple all pouty and pink? Didn't match the right one though, so he pinched the other one.

"I will kill you both."

Damon rumbled, the sound happy. "Fierce lady."

Chase nodded, feeling almost like a pup, eager and tickled, like champagne was running through his veins. The feeling was just bizarre, but he didn't fight it. In fact, he went with it, pushing the tray off onto the bedside table. "Maybe it's time for dessert."

"Dessert? We had waffles." Shanna was studiously lapping her fingers clean.

"Mmm. Dessert is always good." Damon got it. He knelt up, pushing Chase over on his hands and knees. "Start with the lady."

Chase growled happily, pouncing Shanna, face in her soft belly as her nails dug into his scalp. She smelled like musk, like the good perfume most women paid hundreds for. Shanna had it naturally, and he licked at her lower tummy, working down.

"Good boy." Damon patted his ass, and that made him growl. He wanted to bite the man, but then something hard and slick poked his ass, pushing between his cheeks, Damon sliding a thick finger right inside him.

He groaned instead, rubbing his chin against the top of her chestnut curls, the scent of her making everything even headier. Sharp, spicy, she made his mouth water. He bent lower, nipping at the tender inside of her thigh.

"Oh." She sat halfway up, shoulders leaving the mattress. "Stings."

Damon's touch was lighting him up, making him shiver, making him bite her again. He wagged his hips, trying to get more of Damon while he pushed down to taste Shanna's core.

"Chase!" Her cry was all female pleasure.

He slipped his hands under Shanna's ass, tilting her so he could drag his tongue over her folds. Damon gave him another finger, and he stretched out there between them, caught in their web of energy.

His belly pulled up so tight it burned, and he licked and lapped even as his hips moved, hungry for Shanna's sweetness. She squeezed her thighs around his head, holding him there until all he knew was her and the pressure of Damon's fingers inside him.

He heard Damon talking, but the words meant nothing at all. He needed more. He pushed back, demanding, and Damon smacked the backs of his thighs. "I say when, Chase."

That he heard and felt. Fuck. It was like lightning, shooting up along his spine. He wasn't into that. Not. At all. Christ, he hoped Damon didn't stop.

Shanna scratched his shoulders, digging in enough to sting. "That is so damned pretty, him spanking your ass."

He growled softly, deep in his chest, but she didn't sound like she was mocking, not at all. She petted him, soothing the sting of her scratches, her pussy so hot and smooth.

"Need inside you, Chase." Damon's words were a low rumble and he arched his back, unbearably curious, wanting to feel that cock inside him. He'd never wanted anyone the way he wanted these two.

"Gonna let him in, Chase?" Shanna stroked his hair off his forehead. "He's big, and so hot. You'll love it."

Chase just nodded, licking her, sucking at her clit. He'd offered his ass. He wouldn't take it back.

Shanna whimpered softly, her hips rolling. "Oh, fuck. Right there."

He grunted, licking at her moisture, tasting her essence. She was so soft, so open. His thumbs pressed inside her, filling her as Damon's thick heat rubbed against his hole.

They worked together well, him and Damon. He gave Shanna two fingers even as Damon pushed into him, cock just slick enough not to hurt. That cock might split him in two.

Damon took his time, though, rocking into him in slow, careful motions, letting his body adjust. His muscles clenched, then relaxed, and he could lift his head a moment and breathe before working Shanna's clit with his tongue again.

It took them awhile to find a rhythm -- Shanna was quick, hips moving so fast under him, while Damon was just relaxed, easy. Almost lazy. They kept him off guard, his body swaying, his breath coming so fast he started to get dizzy.

Finally though, they synced, finding a pattern to make him short out. He rocked, feeling surrounded, completely out of control. The rush was amazing. Shanna called to him, so vocal, so needy, wild and twisting under him as Damon burned into his fucking bones. His head spun, his body bucking. He used every bit of skill he had with his tongue, flicking it against Shanna, circling her clit while he fucked her cunt with his fingers.

"Chase!" She started coming for him, body shaking violently beneath him, feet drumming on the sheets.

Chase lifted his head, watching her, her skin flushed deep rose, her breasts and belly so beautiful they made him ache.

"Pay attention, Chase." Damon hit his ass, then slapped it again. "Feel me."

"Damon." He keened softly. "Please."

Shanna moved down, impaled herself on his cock and he howled, the world going gray on the edges. He couldn't think, didn't even know if he could move. Thank God Damon started slamming into him, moving for him. Shanna met every thrust with her own strength, fucking herself on him.

Chase needed to come. Had to. Damon kept fucking him like there was no tomorrow, but his balls were gonna bust.

It was Shanna's nails that dragged over his skin one more time, shoving him over the edge. He shouted, his seed bursting from him, filling Shanna up. Chase's body jerked and his ass clenched on Damon's cock. The heat from Damon was overwhelming for a heartbeat, then he breathed through it.

Chase figured he was good until Shanna shook around him, crying out her pleasure. Which triggered Damon's orgasm, wet and so hot inside him that he almost blacked out. Pleasure, not pain. Like that was what he was made for. Shanna's arms were cool compared to Damon, soft where they wrapped around him.

Chase panted, resting on her, licking sweat from her skin. "God Almighty."

Damon was still buried deep, hands like brands on his hips. The man was about to get real heavy, too. Chase wiggled.

"Mmmnph. No moving, man. You'll get me going again."

Chase and Shanna both turned to stare at the man. Amazed.

Damon's skin pinked. "What?"

Shanna's eyebrow arched. "Sizzling hot and premium fuckability."

Chase nodded happily. "We might have to keep him."

"Sounds perfect. We captured you. We get custody." Shanna reached around Chase to poke Damon.

Damon grinned. "I like it. I'll even buy the pho when we finally get out of bed."

Shanna made a happy, yummy little sound. "Good boys."

Eventually they'd have to talk about Damon and the hunters and what the hell was going on with the three of them, but right now, Chase was melted. Content, deep in his bones.

Well-fucked and fine.

Chapter Three

Damon watched his two new lovers sleep.

They were definitely his lovers, not just a one-night stand. He didn't know how or why he'd connected with them like he had, but damn, he was gonna figure out how to stay with them.

Of course, there was the little matter of his job to contend with. A job he was very busy fucking up right now.

Shanna was curled around him, a constant soft sound rumbling in her chest. Chase was sprawled out, snoring like a freight train. The man twitched when he had nightmares, too, howling lightly.

Frickin' adorable.

He thought about going out and seeing if his cell was in the car. It had fallen out of his cargo pants somewhere. Hopefully not at the raid site.

He stretched and Shanna's eyes popped open, staring at him, glowing a bright green. "Hey, lady." He said it quietly, trying not to wake Chase. "You okay?"

"I was dreaming about you." She crawled more firmly on top of him, cheek soft as silk on his skin.

"Were you? What was I doing?" Soft, curvy, she looked so womanly, but there was hard muscle there, too. She worked hard to keep in shape for her job, just like he did.

"Running with us, during the moon."

"No shit? You know I'm not a shifter, right?" He'd read all the government literature, seen the training films.

"I know. It was dreaming. I nap during the moon. A lot."

"Not much of a runner, huh?" He'd bet Chase was full of energy, chasing the moon and howling. Chase snuffled, and Damon laid a hand on that perfect, hard male ass. So pretty, the both of them.

"Why run when you can wait and pounce?"

"Do you climb trees, baby?" He used his free hand to touch her, sliding up and down her back.

"I do." When his fingers found the small of her back, she arched, spine curling impossibly. She was so slinky. So catlike. It fascinated him.

"You'll have to show me sometime," he murmured.

"I can…" She stopped, head tilting. "What was that?"

She leapt from the bed, grabbing a Glock from a holster hanging on the nightstand. "Stay here."

"You're naked."

"You noticed." She grinned, headed for the door. "I like that about you."

"Damn it." No way was he staying here if she'd heard something that made her that worried. This was her territory. She ought to know all the noises.

"Chase? Keep him here." She slipped out the door, closing it behind her.

"Wha? What the fuck?" Chase sat up in bed, looking around wildly. He kept his cool though, and kept his voice down. "What happened?"

Damon stood, hunting his pants. "I don't know, man."

The sound of shots came quick and fast, then the unmistakable pop of a flash bang. Goddamn it.

"Get dressed," Damon spat, hunkering down and looking in drawers for more weapons. "And keep your head down."

A low growl answered him, the biggest fucking wolf he'd ever seen hitting the door. Christ, Chase was just magnificent, and Damon blinked. That was Chase. He really was a fucking werewolf. Another bang sounded and he stumbled back, the lights dazing him. Shit. Shit, don't hurt them.

"Spider? Spider, you in here?"

"Jack?" Damon knew that voice. One-Eyed Jack was a member of his Ops unit, EOS. Christ. "What the hell are you doing here?"

"Saving your sorry ass. Why you naked, cher?" Jack looked him over, one black brow winging up. The other was barely visible over Jack's eyepatch.

"Uh." That was tough to explain. "I was being interrogated and we had sex instead." Okay, not so tough.

"You fucked the critters? Ooo-eee! You a stud. Come on. We go."

"What did you do to them?" He wouldn't leave them if they were hurt, his Chase and Shanna. He would make sure they were safe.

"Tranqed 'em. They just protecting their own. Come on, 'fore I shoot you."

"Bring them inside, at least." He took the cargos and shirt Jack tossed him, sliding them on before digging out his boots from under the bed. God, he didn't want to leave. It was probably best if he did, though.

"Wolf's on the stairs. Little gal is locked in her pantry."

"Huh. She's dangerous, man." He grinned at Jack, already missing his shifters. How fucking crazy was this? "I'm ready. My hunter cell probably thinks I'm dead or compromised, though. My cover is blown."

"You can debrief the colonel at the safe house. He'll want to know everything."

"Yeah. I can." He wanted one last look at Chase and Shanna, but as soon as he left the bedroom his squad fell in on either side of him, hustling him down and out the door.

Looked like it didn't matter how many sparks had flown between him and his pair of shifters. This assignment was over.

Fucking builder.

Thud.

Fucking strong-assed reclaimed wood.

Thud.

Fucking pantry door that would not open no matter how hard she hit it.

Thud.

Fucking locks.

Thud.

Shanna didn't have a single place on her that didn't hurt. She grabbed a can of tuna, screaming at the top of her lungs as she hurled it at the door, furious that she'd gotten herself locked in the goddamned pantry.

"*Fuckers!*"

A thud came from the other side of the door, and she hoped to God one of those freakishly good special ops types was still out there. If they let her out she was going to rip their balls off.

"I want out!" She threw herself at the door, wild to get to Chase, to Damon. Her boys. She couldn't hear them, couldn't feel them.

The door handle rattled. "Shanna?"

Oh. Chase. That was Chase. He sounded tiny, like he'd shrunk. "Let me out, Chase! I'm locked in here! Did they shoot you? Drug you? They drugged me. Is Damon there?"

"I'm trying. There's this plastic lock thing on the handle. Like in a nursing home." The door rattled again. "Damon is gone. I don't -- tranquilizers mess with me, honey." His voice got stronger with every word, though, so there was hope.

"Water. Drink some water." Goddamn it. Seriously? Pups never did as well with drugs.

"Okay. Where are your tools, honey? Your guns are gone."

Her lips tightened. Someone was going to die. "They can't all be gone. Look in the basement."

"I just need a hammer." Oh, he was so not laughing at her. Except it sounded like he was.

"Just open the fucking door, Chase!" She started throwing more cans at the door.

"Okay. Jeez." She heard footsteps, heard him muttering. Then he faded away, obviously heading for the basement. Then he came back, and the sound of him whacking the hell out of the lock. It took him three tries.

By the time the door came open, she'd shifted and leapt out, snarling and spitting.

Chase stumbled back, naked, covered in bruises, the place where the dart had entered his flesh purple and swollen.

She pounced him, sniffing and holding on, vocalizing as she dragged her tongue over his body. Poor wolf. Poor mate. She tilted her head. Mate. Huh. She cleaned him thoroughly, careful of the dart wound.

Still, it needed cleaning, and she held him down until she was satisfied, then she went hunting for their human. She followed the obvious trail out of the cabin to where tire tracks led down the mountain. Two all-terrain type vehicles. Diesel. Damn. She growled, turning back to the house for Chase and that nose.

Like he'd read her mind, he met her at the stairs, his wolf form stunning. He was all gray and gold, pale eyes glinting. He was huge, too, bigger as a wolf than she would have expected.

She headbutted him. *Help. Help. Damon's gone.* Could he hear her? She thought he could.

I know. We'll find him.

Yes. There he was, right there in her head like a mate ought to be. He turned tail and ran, nose to the ground. She followed, protecting his flank, eyes sharp on the shadows. He kept his pace steady, which she appreciated. She was made for bursts of speed, not long treks, and going too fast would wear her down.

They went away from town, not toward it, and she lashed her tail, wondering if these bastards were camping right on her doorstep. They'd kill the fucking hunters and take Damon right back.

He was theirs, after all. Theirs.

Chase didn't seem to be having trouble following the scent. His tail waved like a flag when he turned off the main road, heading up a small canyon.

Excellent. She went up into the trees, leaping to keep up, straining to see. She followed Chase, and it seemed like forever. Fucking forever. Then Chase turned off one more time, following a dirt track.

Shit, she knew this place. An abandoned mine, complete with underground hideout. She chirruped softly, warning her mate. Close. They were close.

Chase slowed, picking his way across the rocks and dirt, not making a sound. Good wolf. He was a better tracker than she'd expected.

She saw a guard, but only one, and she leapt, taking him out silently, batting the man's head against a rock. Chase woofed softly, the sound barely there, and led the way to the little trailer that sat just outside the mineshaft.

She stood up, peering in the window, nostrils working. *Damon? Damon, mate? Are you in there?*

Someone is there. Chase rumbled a little, the growl clear. *We have to get him.*

There are three of them and Damon. You take the front, I'll take the back.

On it. Chase went low to the ground, his tail straight out behind him. Stalking the door.

She ran around the trailer, clenched down, ready to pounce. She just needed to see how small that little window was. She gauged it with her eye. She could make it.

She sent Chase a warning before she leapt, crashing through the window and landing in the middle of a... card game.

Card game?

Chase came slamming through the front door of the place a few seconds later, scrabbling about and going for someone's leg. Three men who weren't Damon leaped up, cursing. The one who was their mate threw himself in front of her. "Don't fucking shoot them!"

"These your pets, Spider?"

She stopped. Stared. Pets? She stilled, stopped for a heartbeat and processed. Cards. Pets. Oh, God.

She'd made a mistake. She'd made a fool out of herself and Chase.

Run, mate. Run.

She headed out like a streak, racing for the trees, the mountains, the darkness.

Somewhere she could hide.

Chase sat on his haunches and blinked at the men, at the tactical gear strewn around and the plate of jalapeno poppers in the tiny toaster oven.

What the flying fuck? Shanna was gone. Chasing her right now would just exhaust him. He'd find her by scent, assuming she didn't just go home. There was no fucking way he was going to pass up giving Damon a piece of his mind.

He shifted in a heartbeat, dropping the wolf like a heavy coat, springing over the table to whack Damon with his balled-up fist. "Pets? Your fucking pets? You played us, you rotten son of a bitch."

Damon stared at him. "Played you? You two kidnapped me!"

Oh, he didn't think so. "You were trying to shoot a bunch of us at a party. I think that counts as extenuating circumstances." He glared at the other men who stood there, mouths open. "What are you, some sort of vigilante group? You don't stink like the other hunters."

"How did you find us?" One of them -- big and buff and blond and looking like he was chiseled from stone, glared at him.

"Hello? Wolf." He sniffed dramatically. "You smell like an asshole."

Damon snorted, and Chase turned his stare back to the

beautiful bastard. "Government agent, my ass. I swear to God, if I wasn't naked and unarmed I would kick your ass. And if they weren't here to shoot me, I would just wolf out and tear your throat out."

"You told them you were with us?" Big, blond and obviously stupid turned toward Damon.

"Oh, shut up. They had me tied to a chair and were threatening to shoot me. Better they knew that than think I was with the hunters." Damon turned to him, spreading his hands. "I didn't set you up. They came for me and I couldn't think of a way to get out of it. I still have a job to do."

Chase was going to boil over. "You suck, man. You really do. I'm going after Shanna. She's real, at least."

"Real? You two are prejudiced against humans."

"You're not just a human." He knew better. He'd seen the riot cuffs melted, had felt that iron poker of a cock inside him. His cheeks went nuclear hot. He'd let this asshole take what no one else had. "You knock yourself out with your job. We do really need you to get those hunters the fuck out of our territory. You come near us again and I will bite you. Hard enough to kill your ass."

He let the human fall away, and he pushed his wolf form out the door.

His girl was out there, hurt and pissed off, and he needed to find her. Luckily, she'd blazed a trail that a blind pit bull with sinus issues could follow, and he put his head down and went after her, careful to watch the roads.

The kind of day he was having, he would totally get hit by a car.

Chapter Four

His squad looked at him, all wearing identical expressions of disapproval. Ice was the one to say what they were all thinking, though. "Jesus, Spider, did you tell them everything about us?"

Damon sighed, shaking his head. "No. I told them I was hunting the hunters and that I worked for the government. That's all."

"They must be really good in bed, eh? Firecrackers." Jack grinned at him, scarred cheek wrinkling.

"You have no idea." He started for the door, his body telling him to go after them. It lit a fire in him, in fact, his skin heating.

"Where the fuck are you going?" Ice growled. "And where the fuck is Case? He's working point."

"Case? He's out here with a bump on his head." But not dead, thank God. "I have to go make this right." He had a new burn phone, new clothes. "I'll call, check in."

"You're just fucking going?" Ice was going to blow a vein.

"His fucking cover's blown, Ice, Colonel needs to reassign him." Little Gig had his back, still, no matter what their fucking history was. "I can find him, anywhere he goes."

"I'll see you." He had a feeling he'd just gotten himself decommissioned, but he didn't care. He had to find Shanna and Chase. He was burning up.

He was on fire and the only thing to quench it was going to be Shanna and Chase.

She ran until she couldn't move another step, curling up in the fork of a tree, licking her paws to soothe her wounded pride.

Stupid.

Stupid, stupid, stupid.

She'd been used. Duped. God, she'd known better than tying it up with those two. Why had she listened to her fucking body not her brain?

Because Damon had been blistering hot and Chase was delicious and she was a sucker.

She chuffed out a sigh, letting her tail flick out her irritation. Eventually, she'd have to find her way home.

She'd sleep and then pack and head up into the mountains for a few months. Lick her wounds. Avoid males of all types. Chase probably didn't deserve to be abandoned like Damon did, but she needed to make a clean break.

She'd been the one to go after Damon, anyway, right? Chase was probably pissed at her for getting him into this whole mess. Shanna was just about to sink into a real funk and have a pity party when a sharp bark from the base of the tree made her jump half out of her skin.

She leaned down, staring. *What? Go away.*

God, her mate's nose was amazing. He'd followed her all this way, and hadn't confused the trail she'd made on the way to the mine. Chase was stunning.

Come down. His inner voice sounded so peeved.

No. Her butt hurt.

I can't come up. He slapped his paws against the tree.

She knew that. Still, he didn't look like he was going anywhere, so she climbed down, gingerly. Her butt really did hurt, all the way to the end of her tail.

Chase came right to her and cleaned her whiskers, licking gently.

I'm so sorry. She was so ashamed. She'd thought… Chase knew what she'd thought.

Chase nuzzled her again, then shifted, his bruises fading

now, his body shining in the mountain light. "Talk to me, lady. I'm not ready to give up on you."

She climbed into his lap, nuzzling his jaw, mouthing him a little bit as she shifted.

"There you are." He smiled before he kissed her. Then he rested his forehead against hers. "I'm sorry."

"Me too." She curled around him, holding on tight, snuggling. They were hidden from any road by the trees, in a good safe spot. They could just love on each other before tucking tail and heading home.

She didn't know if he had to go back to the pack. Hell, she didn't know anything right now. Well, that wasn't true. She knew Chase was right there, smooth skin against hers. She also knew there was an all-terrain vehicle headed their way.

"Someone's coming." She was going to scream, she was too tired to run.

"They'll just have to run over us." Chase chuckled, the puff of air stirring the hair at her temple.

"Okay. Maybe they won't see us at all."

"Nah. With our luck they'll swerve to miss us and crack up on a tree and we'll have to help them."

The vehicle did head right for them, but stopped about six feet short. The tall, dark man who got out was unmistakable. Damon.

"So, now we're going to commune with nature naked?" Damon asked, stalking toward them.

"Go away." *Okay, move. You have to move.*

"Nope. Get in the Humvee." He stared at them, making her want to hit him. Too bad lactic acid buildup had her muscles weak as a kitten's.

"Fuck off," Chase rumbled, growling low.

She couldn't even shift. All her reserves were gone. Fucking body. Right now she just wanted to bite Damon's leg off.

"Look, I didn't play you guys."

Damon sucked at listening, possibly at following orders. He

was supposed to be a soldier, right? He came over and knelt next to them, reaching out to touch each of them with one hand.

She pulled away, but she couldn't avoid the touch, the connection like lightning in the back of her brain. The spark lit up her nerves, actually giving her some energy back.

"Pets. Your cronies called us pets." Chase was still growling, but Shanna felt the way he leaned into Damon's touch.

"They didn't know."

"You weren't going to tell them. They locked me in my pantry!"

"I thought you'd be better off if I went. I really did." Damon looked right into her eyes, unsmiling, serious. "It's not gonna work, though."

"Just go play soldiers. I… I'm tired." And that was the truth. It had been the longest twelve hours in recorded history.

"No. I'll take you home. Come on." Damon tugged her up like she weighed nothing, hauling Chase to his feet as well.

Damon was warm, solid, and the heat sank into her, making her tingle and ache deliciously. His arm felt like a steel band around her waist as he lifted her, carrying her with no effort at all.

"Be good to her. She's my mate." Chase stayed close, constantly touching her.

"Yeah, well, you two can't be all matey without me." Damon plonked her ass down in the big vehicle and yanked Chase inside, too.

She curled up in Chase's lap. "He sounds sure for a puny human."

Chase nodded, lips on her neck. "He does. He's not just human."

Damon slid into the backseat with them instead of driving them anywhere. "I really thought it would be better if I left. You came to rescue me, though. That's pretty intense."

"You're ours. We wouldn't let someone hurt you."

Chase nodded. "Even if you don't want us, really."

Damon glared at both of them. "Don't be idiots. I came after you, didn't I? Walked right out on my squad."

"Guilt makes people do stupid things."

"Guilt for what!" Damon grabbed them both by the upper arms and shook. "You kidnapped me and jumped me while I was tied to a chair. Forgive me if I wasn't sure exactly what to do when rescue showed up."

"You shot at me!" She roared and pounced him, shaking him hard, leaving Chase to scrabble and yelp behind her.

Damon made this noise, half "urk", half hum of pleasure. "I did not! I was naked in your bedroom."

"You were! You were naked and you're a fucker, making us worry about you!" She leaned down and bit him hard, right on the shoulder, and her body went white-hot with need. Her nipples drew up hard, and her cunt went liquid, hot and wet.

"Oh, God." Chase crowded up against them. "Please."

"Sweet sluts, the pair of you." The words were fond, warm, a tease, but she still bit him again. He deserved it.

Chase growled, and bit Damon, too, which made their very hot human jump and moan. It took less than thirty seconds for Damon to be as naked as she and Chase after that, his cock hard and curving up toward his belly.

They all three slammed together, touching and biting, rubbing and moaning. Chase was wild, and the sounds coming from his human throat were pure wolf. Damon was steaming up the cab of the vehicle, skin so heated she could barely touch him.

She could touch, though, and she'd dare a human to wrap their hand around that blistering cock. She stroked him, up and down, and Chase pushed a hand down to help her. This was gonna take two.

Shanna leaned in, took a hard, sharp kiss from Damon, then Chase. They both kissed her back with fervor, then went after each other, all bitey faces and hot lips. So yummy. They took all of her good sense and threw it out the window.

"This is a terrible idea." She bit Chase's ear, tugged.

Chase groaned. "Awful."

Damon thrust into their hands, panting. "Fucking perfect."

"Mate." His scent filled her nose, rich and sharp and right.

"Yeah. That." Chase laughed, the sound utterly joyful. He pulled her hand away from Damon's cock, then lifted her to slide up over the man's lap.

She leaned back to kiss Chase even as Damon's cock pushed deep inside her. Her men. One filled her, the other held her open, lips on the back of her neck. She moaned, body clenching, gripping around Damon's prick. Chase pushed her down hard, then helped her up. Damon nodded, grinning, looking feral as hell.

"Boys." Oh, fuck. So hot. So deep. So deep inside her.

"Shanna." Damon said her name like it was a prayer, and she believed him, that he hadn't meant to hurt her.

"That's right. That's right, mates. Smell so good." Chase was moaning, panting against them.

"Help me, Chase." Damon moved faster, reaching past her to grab Chase's shoulders.

Chase rubbed against her ass, strong arms moving her, fucking her on Damon's cock. They surrounded her, made her feel protected and safe. They were so beautiful, so hot. Damon was like a machine.

My beautiful girl. Damon's voice poured over her nerves like a splash of whiskey.

She cried out, hearing his words in her head. Yes, he really was a part of them. One of their mates. Oh, God.

They tumbled over, one after another, one orgasm crashing into another and another. She had no idea where she ended and they began by the time they all slumped together, panting, the air in the cab of the vehicle so humid her hair was curling up around her head.

She rested between her men, clinging to them. "So what do we do now?" she finally asked, sucking in deep lungfuls of air.

Chase hummed. "Be mates?"

Shanna grinned and whapped him. "That's a given. I mean practical reality."

Damon snorted. "I don't think this is practical. I'll stay and help with the hunters and we figure this thing out between us."

"You do have a great house, Shanna." Chase nuzzled in.

"Are you saying you want to move in with me, you two?" Was she ready for that? Just like this?

Damon nodded, and so did Chase. So eager.

"Well, I guess we can work it out." She was a little eager herself.

Damon kissed her hard on the mouth, then kissed Chase. "We'll figure it out. I'm a wellspring of information, even if I did just quit my job. I'll have to call the guys, make sure they know I don't need rescuing."

Shanna laughed out loud, giving him an intimate little squeeze. "Nope. No rescue. You're not being hunted. You're firmly trapped now. Mated."

This might be a really bad idea, but it was going to be one hell of a ride.

Julia Talbot lives in the great Southwest, where there is hot and cold running rodeo, cowboys, and everything from meat and potatoes to the best Tex-Mex. A full-time author, Julia has been published by Dreamspinner Press, Samhain, and Changeling Press. She believes that everyone deserves a happy ending, so she writes about love without limits, where boys love boys, girls love girls, and boys and girls get together to get wild, especially when her crazy paranormal characters are involved. Find Julia at @juliatalbot on Twitter, or at www.juliatalbot.com.